VIRTUALLY
UNDETECTABLE

LIBBY FISCHER HELLMANN

THE RED HERRINGS PRESS
CHICAGO, IL

This book was originally published as part of the High-Tech Crime Solvers series.

Names: Hellmann, Libby Fischer

Title: VIRTUALLY UNDETECTABLE / Libby Fischer Hellmann

978-1-7364528-3-7 (Ebook)

978-1-7364528-3-7 (Print)

Chapter 1

The woman who started it all swept into the bank during lunch. In her early forties, she looked like one of those women who'd made it and wanted everyone to know. She wore a woven, gold and brown Chanel suit with simple gold jewelry. It fit her well; she was gracefully slim and her Louboutin shoes added four inches to her height. Her perfectly dyed blond hair was tightly wound in a bun. Her make-up was expertly applied, and her nails sported dark brown polish to complement the suit.

Rachel Foreman, who was covering for the other three lobby managers, absorbed the woman's presence right away. As she approached she gave Rachel a smile that exuded quiet power and confidence. Rachel, on the other hand, felt a pang of anxiety, the same pang she'd felt about one or two professors in college whose reputations commanded instant respect. Rachel wanted to please this woman.

Rachel flashed what she hoped was a competent smile. "Good afternoon. How can I help you?"

The woman sat at Rachel's desk. The scent of Chanel No. Five drifted over Rachel. Classy. The woman shrugged off her suit jacket.

April in Chicago was iffy, but this morning had been warm and breezy, promising more of the same. It wouldn't last.

"I'd like to open a new credit card account," she said.

"I can help you with that," Rachel said. "Do you have an account with us?"

"Several." She reeled off a string of numbers. "That's my checking."

Rachel scribbled them down. "Just a sec.'" She punched in the numbers and waited. The computer returned an account held by Pamela N. Cannon.

"Ms. Cannon," Rachel said.

"That's right."

"Your name sounds familiar."

The woman shrugged. Rachel took it as a sign not to pursue the matter. She punched up another screen on her computer. "We work through a third party, so we'll need some information from you for the application. The good news is that we can often get approval within minutes."

The woman nodded.

Rachel asked for her full name, address, phone numbers, date and place of birth. Ms. Cannon replied promptly with all the required information. "I'll need the numbers of your other accounts with us, but I'll look them up. She tabbed to other screens, copied what she needed, including the woman's Social Security number, and clicked back to the application to fill it in. When she got to approximate income she asked, "Your income, please?"

"Seven million, most of it invested," the woman replied in a soft voice.

Jesus Christ! Rachel suppressed her reaction. Pamela Cannon was loaded. Who was she? And why did she need yet another credit card? Of course, that was none of her business.

"And the net worth of your investments, if you have any?"

"About thirty. Million."

Rachel was speechless. It was all she could do to nod. She finished by asking her Social, and her mother's maiden name.

The woman shifted forward in her chair. "Could I see that you entered the correct Social Security number? You can't be too careful these days."

Rachel frowned. Technically, she was not supposed to let customers see their data. Even their own Social Security numbers. For exactly the same reason the woman had just offered. "I'm sorry, but it's against policy for just that reason. But you're welcome to tell me what it is and I'll verify the number." She paused. "I have a feeling you'll be approved in a minute anyway."

Rachel's phone rang. She looked around, saw she was still the only manager on the floor. "I'm sorry, I need to get this." She picked up the phone. "Rachel Foreman." She frowned. "For me?" She listened to the voice on the phone. "I'll be there in ten minutes." More silence. "Now? Are you sure?" She sighed. "Okay."

Rachel minimized her screen and told the woman, "Apparently, there's a document at the front for me which I need to get right away. I apologize. I'll be right back."

"That's okay," Pamela Cannon said. "I understand."

Two minutes later, Rachel returned with a manila envelope. She smiled at her customer and scanned her desk and screen. Everything seemed to be where she had left it. Pamela drummed her polished nails on the arm of the chair.

Rachel finished inputting the information and clicked on 'submit.' "All done. Let's see what happens."

Within a minute, the screen flashed. "APPROVED." Rachel smiled. "See? You've been approved, ma'am. Your card will be mailed to you in ten business days. Is there anything else I can do for you today?"

Ms. Cannon shook her head. "Not today. You've been most helpful. Thanks a lot, Rachel Foreman."

Rachel startled, then realized the woman was reading her name on the corner of her desk.

"Don't hesitate to call if you have any questions."

The woman got up, pulled her jacket on, and strolled to the front exit. It was then it came to Rachel. Pamela Cannon was the CEO of

Carefill, a major pharmaceutical company headquartered in Chicago. Although the name of the parent company wasn't well known, they had developed several famous drugs, including the most popular anti-anxiety medication on the market, a pill that eliminated stomach ulcers, and several promising cancer drugs. Carefill was said to be in the same league as Abbott and Baxter. Rachel's mother, Ellie Foreman, had produced a video for the company several years ago.

Rachel couldn't wait to tell her mother Pamela Cannon had come into the bank today and what she had done for her. But first, she opened the manila envelope. It was empty. How strange. She turned it over. No return address or name. What the hell was going on?

Rachel's mood darkened. Something wasn't right. It happened just when she was inputting Cannon's Social Security number. Suspicious by nature—her mother had taught her that, and experience had borne it out—she searched Google for Pamela Cannon and gasped.

The woman who came into the bank slid into a Mercedes idling at the curb.

"How'd it go?" the driver adjusted his rear view. "You get it?"

The woman smiled. "No squeaky wheel here."

"Did the call come at the right time?"

"Perfect. Now let's get out of here."

The Mercedes pulled around a truck in front of them and sped across Washington Street.

Chapter 2

The female CEO in the photo on Carefill's website was not the woman who came into the bank. They were similar, both with blond hair in a bun, Chanel suits, and modest jewelry, but the real Pamela Cannon looked at least ten years older than the woman who applied for a credit card. The real Pamela Cannon's face was lined, tired-looking, and thicker.

Rachel couldn't do any work and spent the rest of the lunch hour tapping her fingers on her desk. As soon as the other managers were back, she headed to her boss's office. As bosses went, Robert Katz was a pretty good one. He was in his fifties, balding, and wore rimless glasses, which, though they were back in fashion, always slipped from the bridge of his nose. Rachel suspected he had hit the high point of his career and was satisfied with it. In fact, when she knocked at the door, already open a crack, she heard his executive chair squeak as if he'd been leaning back. Napping, perhaps?

He cleared his throat. "Come on in."

"Hi, Bob. We have a problem."

∼

When Rachel finished explaining, Bob cancelled the card online, then told her to follow him. Together they took the elevator up to the Bank Secrecy Act unit, AKA the Fraud Department

The head of the department, Eric Arnall, a fortyish redhead with glasses and piercing blue eyes that immediately made Rachel feel uncomfortable buzzed his female assistant. They all moved to a conference room where Arnall asked her to walk him through the entire transaction. When she got to the Social Security number and the emergency package, Arnall stopped her.

"Wait a minute. Let's go over that again. First, what time was it?"

"I—I'm not sure. About one twenty, I guess."

"Okay. Now what did she say? Exactly."

"She asked if she could see it to make sure it was correct."

"And you said..."

"That it wasn't possible. But if she wanted to tell me, I'd verify it for her."

"Ok. Then what happened?"

"I got a call from the front. They said I had a package. I tried to say I'd come in ten minutes but they said it was a priority. I had to come right now."

"Who called?"

"I thought it was a receptionist. Or the guard out front. It was an internal call."

"Male or female?"

"Male."

Arnall frowned, and when he did, Rachel saw deep furrows on his brow. "You didn't ask who it was?"

"No."

"Why not?"

"It didn't seem necessary."

Arnall's crossed his arms. "Okay. Then what?"

Now that she was repeating what happened, the timing seemed awfully convenient—too convenient. "I got up and went to the lobby entrance where the package was. The guy behind—"

Arnall cut her off. "You used Control-L, right?"

"I'm sure I did."

"Really? Think about it. There's something off. If you did, there shouldn't be any way she could have seen your screen."

Rachel bit her lip. "I thought I locked it. Then again, I was only going to be gone for a minute. I use Control-L if I'm going to a meeting or lunch or at the end of the day. But for this, maybe I didn't..." Rachel's voice trailed off.

Bob, Arnall, and the female assistant stared at her, disapproval washing across their faces. Every employee was taught to use Control-L if they ever had to leave their desks for any amount of time. But most employees, if they were going to the washroom, or to get a cup of coffee, just minimized their screens. It was easier.

Except, Rachel realized with sudden terror, the woman had somehow walked around to her computer, unminimized her screen, and stolen Pamela Cannon's Social Security number. Rachel's stomach clenched. She'd screwed up big time. She started to feel nauseous.

Arnall confirmed her blunder with a sigh. "So, that's how it happened."

Rachel kept her mouth shut. What could she possibly say? Guilt and shame poured over her.

"Okay. Bob, you call Cannon. Tell her what happened. Tell her it's important for her to file a police report."

"Is that really necessary? I cancelled the transaction. The card won't be coming through."

"But someone has her Social Security number."

"Someone has everybody's number these days," Bob said. Rachel knew he was trying to defend her. She wasn't sure he should.

Arnall shook his head. "Cannon's a valued customer. What if she pulls out of the bank altogether?"

"That's what I'm saying," Bob continued. "Maybe it's not necessary."

"And what if the thieves are caught and admit they got the number from our bank? From a careless bank employee who couldn't be bothered to Control-L her screen? We can't take that chance."

"Wait a minute," Bob said. "That's not fair, Eric. Rachel only did what most employees do. I've even done it once or twice."

"Well, then, perhaps it's time for a new training program. That kind of thing just can't happen."

"There's something else. You know over fifty percent of people whose information is hacked don't bother to file police reports. They don't think it will make a damn bit of difference. A woman like Pamela Cannon probably doesn't think it's worth her time. I'm not sure I do, either, since there was no dollar loss." Bob pushed his glasses back up his nose. "I'll offer her a year of credit monitoring, of course."

"She probably already has it. But she's an important VIP. What else can we do?" Arnall glanced around the room. No one answered.

"OK. Let's think about it. Please, Bob. Try to get her to file a police report." He turned to his assistant. "You get the tapes and we'll take a look. Maybe we'll see something before we hand them over to CPD." He pointed to Rachel. "You can leave." He turned to Bob. "Find out who her personal banker is and have him come up here."

Arnall was businesslike. He wasn't unkind, and Bob didn't think it was a big deal. But the knot in the pit of her stomach told Rachel there would be hell to pay.

Chapter 3

W hen Pamela Cannon got Bob Katz's phone call, she was in the middle of an executive meeting. She had told Kelly, her assistant, not to interrupt her unless it was an emergency. Kelly put the call through.

"This is Pamela Cannon."

"Ms. Cannon, this is Robert Katz from Midwest Mutual Bank. I have some potentially bad news." He explained the situation. "We want you to know we have cancelled the transaction, and there will be no dollar loss at all, but there is the remote chance that someone now has your Social Security number." He further explained that they would offer her a year's worth of monitoring through Kroll. If someone tried to use her social, she would know instantly. "So. Even though the situation has been managed, we strongly encourage you to file a police report."

"A police report?" She scoffed. 'I'll think about it, but we both know they're not going to find anything. And they have a lot more important things to do, anyway."

"Well, without a police report, we can't really do much more than we have. If you file one, we can be more pro-active. So can the police. Scanning videos, getting prints, widening their investigation."

"Tell me something, Mr. Katz. If this happened to you, and you were me, would you file a report?"

He hesitated. "Yes. I would."

"That doesn't sound like a ringing endorsement. I'm inclined to just let it go. How did you happen to discover it?"

Again Katz hesitated. "After one of our managers took the card information in your name, she compared her to a photo of you on Google and realized it wasn't you."

"How enterprising of her." Pamela chuckled. "Well, please thank her. I appreciate what you've done. Hopefully, this will be the end of it." She hung up and turned to the other two men in her office.

"What was that about a police report?" one of the men asked.

Pamela shrugged, touched her blond hair, and smoothed the skirt of her Michael Kors suit. "Apparently the bank thinks someone tried to apply for a credit card in my name and managed to steal my Social Security number. Why do you ask, Devin?"

Devin McDuff, tall and gangly, looked awkward in a suit and tie. Pamela always pictured her Director of IT and Internal Security as the guy with the pocket protector. Which he was once upon a time. Now he and the other man exchanged a glance.

"What?" She massaged her left wrist with her fingers. Her arthritis was acting up today. "Why are you trading looks?"

"Devin's right. It's not a trivial matter," the other man said. Stan Trollop, Carefill's COO, looked like a "proper" executive in his bespoke suit, shined shoes, and reading glasses perched on his head. "Especially in light of what we've been discussing."

"Oh, come on, Stan," Pamela said with a flick of her good hand. "You can't possibly believe this has something to do with the Project."

"To be honest, we don't know," Devin said. "Still, not a great idea to treat it so casually. Do you know what someone can do with your social?"

Pamela shook her head.

"Well, let's start with the thief declaring she lost her wallet and showing up at the DMV to get a new driver's license with her picture and address but your name. Once she has that, she can go to the post office and get your mail redirected to a new address. Then she might apply for a new passport in your name. She could also reroute your bank accounts, after she emptied them. Oh, yes. And she could add a new phone number to the accounts so all the statements would go to her. And that's just the start."

Pamela felt the color drain from her face. "I suppose I never thought about it that way."

"It already has to other people. Do you want me to show you some articles?"

She hesitated, then shook her head. "I believe you. You're my VP of Security. You would know."

Chapter 4

"Hello?" Ellie Foreman picked up the phone that night.

"Mom? It's me." Rachel sipped a glass of white wine.

"Hi, me. What's going on?"

"You know that woman, Pamela Cannon, at Carefill? You produced a video for them a few years ago?"

"I remember," Ellie said.

"Well, she's back. And I may get fired because of her."

"What?"

Rachel explained what happened at the bank, the meeting with Bob, then Arnall. Ellie listened. When Rachel stopped, Ellie asked, "Did you watch the video they brought back to the conference room?"

"Yes."

"And it wasn't the real Pamela Cannon."

"Right."

"Can you get a copy of it? The surveillance video?"

"Why?"

"Do you want to keep your job?"

"Of course."

"Well, I have an idea that might help."

"What is it? Your ideas are sometimes pretty weird."

"Just get a copy of the tape. I'll tell you later."

"I'm not senior enough."

"What about your boss. Bob something or other?"

"I don't know if *he's* senior enough, either."

"Didn't you say Bob talked to her, and she seemed okay?"

"Yeah, but I don't believe it. I screwed up big time when I didn't Control-L the screen."

Ellie was quiet for a minute. Then, "Look, honey. You didn't do anything that anyone else hasn't. Don't be so hard on yourself. I'm sure this will blow over."

"I don't know. I have a bad feeling about this. I'll talk to you later." Rachel hung up.

Ellie had a bad feeling about it too, but she wouldn't tell Rachel. Yet.

Rachel was at her desk the next morning when she saw Eric Arnall and another man go into Bob's office and close the door. She tensed and waited. It wasn't long. A few minutes later, Arnall and the man with him exited Bob's office and disappeared. A moment after that Bob shuffled out and headed towards her.

"Bad news," Bob said when he was within earshot.

She looked up. "How bad?"

"As bad as it gets."

"Oh, god." Her fist swept up to her mouth.

"Cannon thought about it overnight and changed her mind. She filed a police report this morning. And she talked with the president of the bank." Bob hesitated. "About you."

Rachel tightened her lips so much they seemed to disappear.

"There was some talk of pressing charges, and—"

"What? Against me? For what?"

"For not following the rules. But we talked her out of that. Well, Arnall did."

"Oh no, Bob." Rachel's voice shot up an octave. "Oh no. I've never been fired."

"There's always a first time. Hey, this isn't such a great place to work, anyway. Look, they have this form you're supposed to sign." He dropped it onto her desk.

Rachel picked it up. "What is it?" She started reading out loud. When she got to "confirms the termination," she stopped and stared at Bob. "They want me to admit I was fired?"

"It's some kind of legal mumbo-jumbo. But you need to sign it. Then—"

"What if I don't? Will they un-fire me?"

He gave her a half-smile, half-grimace. "No one I know has chosen not to sign."

Rachel shook her head. "Jeezus." She scrawled her name on the bottom of the sheet.

"Now, get your things together. They want you out of here in an hour. I'll walk you out."

"But, isn't there someone I can talk to? Can I call Pamela Cannon and explain? Apologize? My mother—"

Bob shook his head. "I'm sorry Rachel."

He brought her a cardboard box, and Rachel started to pack up her things. She recalled her mother asking about a copy of the bank's surveillance tape. "Bob, there's a last favor I need to ask."

Chapter 5

The woman who stole Cannon's Social Security number from the bank sipped a glass of wine in a booth at Clyde's, an upscale bar on Rush Street. It featured a lot of polished wood, gold accents, and a private cigar room in the back for old white men who were pretending they were still powerful.

A man, late forties, she guessed, sat across from her. He was dressed casually in jeans and a hoodie, which made the two an odd pair, since she was all business in a gray St. John's suit, pearls, and matching bag.

"So where do we go from here?" the man asked.

"Part Two," the woman replied. "Do not pass go. Do not collect two hundred dollars." She laughed. "I always thought it should be two thousand."

"Come on."

The woman's smile faded, and she straightened up. "We'll get a driver's license in her name. We'll open a bank account at Chase and slowly transfer funds from her Midwest Mutual account. We'll get a couple of new credit cards, Visa, AmEx. All perfectly legal, by the way." She took another sip. "We're still not sure about the passport."

"What?"

"We were thinking we might set up offshore. That would make it harder for the Feds. You know, forcing them to work with foreign law enforcement systems and all. But we haven't decided yet." She picked up her bag and rummaged through it. "We have time."

"Hey," the man said. "You know I don't have unlimited resources."

She pulled out a lipstick. "We understand, Mr. Fields. But remember, we told you the entire project could take six months. You said you could live with that."

"That's still the time frame, right?"

She reached into the bag again and pulled out a tiny mirror. "We're right on schedule. Within a couple weeks we'll start spending on the cards and pay them off with the new bank account. We don't want to attract any attention. I'll be an upstanding law-abiding woman. I mean, she *is* Pamela Cannon."

"When do I meet your partner?"

She started to apply the lipstick. "When the time is right."

"What does that mean?"

"We're planning to do a dry run of the operation in about a month. We figured you'd want to be a part of it. You'll meet him then."

"Tell me about it."

She blotted her lips and dropped the lipstick and mirror back into her bag. "That's the fun part. We buy a plane ticket in her name. Make a reservation at a nice hotel. Rent a car. I show up wherever we've decided to stage it, but disappear in a hurry a few days later. All hell will break loose."

"You're not using fake credit card accounts or anything, right? I read this article about two brothers who—"

Irritation flashed across the woman's face. "We're not bush league, Mr. Fields. I told you that."

"You told me a lot of things, Jennifer." He shifted. "And please. Call me Don."

"Well Don, we're way past skimming card numbers off the dark web." She sat back in the booth. "Tell me something. Why were you fired from Carefill?"

"How did you know that?"

She flashed him a patronizing glance. "Did you really think we didn't do due diligence on you before we took the assignment?"

He returned her gaze, broke eye contact, and shrugged. "They called it non-performance issues."

"What does that mean?"

"I'd rather not go into it. It's none of your business anyway."

"Oh, but you're wrong. It *is* our business. We're taking a huge risk working with you."

He squinted and said, "If you already know I got fired, I'll bet you sure as shit know why."

Touché. She'd been testing him. She glanced at her phone. "Sorry, I need to go. I'll be in touch in a week or so about the dry run. Stay cool, my friend."

"Easy for you to say."

The woman hesitated for a moment. She hoped her face was unreadable. Then she rose from the booth. "Thanks for the drink."

Don muttered under his breath. "I know Jennifer's not your real name."

She headed toward the door but not before arching an eyebrow at him over her shoulder.

Chapter 6

Rachel opened her Evanston apartment's front door to find her mother with a pizza in one hand and a bottle of wine in the other. The sight and smell prompted a fresh round of tears. Ellie set everything down onto Rachel's kitchen counter, went to her daughter, and pulled her into her arms.

"It's okay, sweetheart. Really, it is. You are still the best daughter in the world and I love you to the moon and back."

Rachel wailed. "I screwed up. I didn't lock my screen. But nobody does if they're just going to pee or get a cup of coffee. How was I supposed to know the woman would steal Pamela Cannon's social?"

"I know, I know." Ellie rubbed her daughter's back and held her tightly. "But it doesn't mean you're a failure."

"How do you know? I'm thirty years old, Mom. I don't have a career. Or a boyfriend. Or any money to speak of. What's wrong with me?"

"Nothing's wrong with you, honey. You just haven't found something and someone to love. But you will. I promise. And don't forget, you were suffering from PTSD for a couple of years. It takes time to get your mojo back."

"I realize that. I made a mistake going to the police academy. I thought it would solve all my problems."

"It was not a mistake. Not by any stretch of the imagination. No experience in your life is ever wasted. You'll see. It will all come together for you at some point, and when that happens, you'll wonder why you didn't figure it out sooner."

Rachel drew back, a skeptical look on her face. "I don't know. You were already working in TV news by the time you were thirty."

"Yeah, and I got fired, too."

Rachel stiffened and stepped back. "Really? You never told me that."

"Sure, I did."

"No, you didn't." She sniffed again, but her tears stopped. "Maybe you thought you did."

Ellie gazed at her daughter, her curly blond hair, bright blue eyes, tall willowy figure. She was a beautiful young woman, but her beauty was muted tonight by guilt and shame. "Well, let's nuke the pizza, and I'll tell you."

Ten minutes later, her mother dished out thin crust pizza with bacon and mushrooms, Rachel's favorite toppings. She opened the white wine, poured half the bottle into two glasses, and dropped an ice cube into each. She passed one glass to Rachel and took a long sip from her own.

"So I was working at Channel Two as a field producer. I got a lead from a friend who told me a popular restaurant downtown, Mama Linguini's, actually, had been shut down for all sorts of violations. Rats in the kitchen, no hairnets, lack of sanitary facilities for employees... you name it. Turned out the head of the Chicago Department of Public Health had a hard-on for the owner."

"Hard on?" Rachel twirled a long strand of mozzarella around her finger. "What do you mean?"

"The owner was Italian. He had a grown daughter. Apparently the

Public Health director and the daughter had been an item, but they broke up. There were bad feelings on both sides. The director saw this was a way to get retribution."

Rachel frowned. "What does that have do to with your job?"

"I'm getting there. We didn't know they'd been seeing each other. We were doing a series of investigative reports on Chicago restaurants. The reporter was Deb Parker. I was thrilled to be working with her. She was a huge name at the time. Brought in high ratings with every story. So we set up a shoot at the restaurant. We knew it would be closed but she was going to do a stand-up outside, calling them out for their violations, and making the case that consumers had to be careful when choosing a restaurant."

"So?"

"When we got there, the door was wide open, and there were people inside eating lunch. Talk about being surprised. Since I was the one who'd planned the shoot, they turned to me. Deb was really pissed. 'What's going on? I thought the place was shut down.'

"'It was,' I said. 'I don't know what's happening.' 'Well,' she says in this arrogant, you're-nothing-but-a-piece-of-crap tone, 'I think you better find out.' So I went inside. Of course, the aroma of garlic and olive oil hit me right away, but I couldn't enjoy it because the owner's daughter was floating from table to table, *balabussing* everyone in the place. Then I saw her wave her left hand. A huge diamond ring sparkled on her ring finger."

Rachel's mouth opened. "They made up?"

"The father, who, of course, was connected, paid off the public health director. Suddenly, all the health violations disappeared, and the public health director proposed." She took a slice of pizza. "Apparently they'd been negotiating and the amount the father offered wasn't enough, so he upped his offer and tossed in his daughter for good measure."

"So did everyone live happily ever after?"

"Not everyone. Deb—God forbid anyone called her Debbie—was livid. She thought I'd made the whole thing up just to get at *her*, and she complained to the news director. It was me or her, she told him. Guess who got the heave-ho?"

"But you were just as surprised as everyone else!"

"That didn't matter. Deb was everybody's sweetheart. A real prima donna. Pulling in big bucks. Back then they catered to her every wish."

"She's not there now?"

"No. She was fired a few years later. TV news reporters have the life span of a gnat."

Rachel chewed her pizza. "That's so unfair."

"Kind of like your situation, isn't it?"

"Kind of." Rachel finished chewing and swallowed. "You never told me this story before."

"I was probably still ashamed. Which is why I'm telling you now. It wasn't my fault then, and it's not your fault now. Life sometimes turns out that way. But it has a happy ending. I hung out a shingle for myself and own what's now a thriving video production company." She laughed. "At least, sometimes."

"I guess. But I still want to be exonerated, you know?"

"I get it." Ellie smiled. "And if you want, I'll try and help."

"How? I mean, what can you do? Call up Pamela Cannon and tell her what a wonderful daughter I am?"

"No." She took a long swig of wine. "But we can make this work."

Rachel arched an eyebrow. "Should I be worried? Don't forget, I know you pretty well."

"No way." Ellie raised her hands in mock surrender. "Did you manage to get a copy of the surveillance footage inside the bank?"

Rachel stared at her mother, then grinned.

Chapter 7

Josie, aka Jennifer, pulled up to a red brick ranch house with white trim in Mt. Prospect and parked her car. She took her time retrieving a couple of shopping bags with pricy Gold Coast store logos on them and strolled across the lawn to the front door.

Inside, the house was nothing like its prim, unremarkable exterior. The furniture consisted of a few chairs, mostly executive office chairs on casters. Two tables crowded with computer set-ups, a phalanx of cables, and small boxes flashing green or red occupied most of the living room. A man in a Bears t-shirt and jeans hunched over one of the computers. His full head of brown hair was streaked with gray, and he wore reading glasses. Behind the glasses were a pair of suspicious brown eyes that missed nothing.

On another table were dozens of rubber molds and plastic resin used to manufacture credit card skimming devices; skimmers, ATM overlays, and pinhole cameras. There was also a credit card embosser, encoder, and magnetic stripe reader used to create counterfeit cards. Sheets of Illinois state identification holograms as well as an identification card printer used to create fake ID's were set up on yet another table.

Josie walked to the man and massaged his neck. He reached a

hand up and caressed her hand. Looking at the screen over his shoulder, she watched as he scrolled through a website that offered datasets of credit cards. She shook her head. "I thought we weren't doing that anymore. Bigger and better and all that."

"You're right. I just thought I'd pick up a dataset just for odds and ends."

"They're only available for an hour or so, right?"

"Right. One-time use only." He swiveled in the chair, cupped her face with his hands, and kissed her. "I missed you."

"I was meeting with our client." She smiled flirtatiously. "Are you jealous?"

"Always."

Disentangling from his embrace, she sauntered around the computer set up and picked up a manual with the title *How To Commit Identity Theft And Credit Card Fraud.* "He wants to meet you."

He threw her a sharp glance. "You didn't say anything about me, did you?"

"Not a word."

He nodded. "When we're ready, you'll call him and tell him to meet you in Miami." He entered a chat room and started scrolling the conversations. "Shit. Things are busy tonight. Must have been a breach somewhere."

"Hey, baby. Can you stop for a few minutes?"

"Why? Something bothering you?"

Her smile had faded. "Do you ever worry if we can actually pull this off?"

"Nope, not at all. Because we can," Steve answered. "And we will." He inclined his head. "Why? Other than curiosity? Everything okay with Donny boy?"

"He's just antsy. Wants to get on with it." She paused. "Actually, so do I."

Steve smiled. "Then you'll be happy to know the credit cards we applied for a couple of weeks ago arrived today. And they're perfectly legal. I changed your contact email and phone, and I'll switch the address next week. Have to do these things slowly so we don't attract attention. But you'll have to swing by the DMV downtown for a new driver's license."

"Under her current address?"

"Right."

"Did you get proof of residency?"

He picked up a piece of paper. "Right here. Was able to print out her most recent ComEd bill."

"Perfect!" She ran her tongue around her lips. "But I'm getting impatient. You sure we need to wait?"

"Listen, Josie, our plan is ingenious because it's legal. Mostly. We go slow and we lay low. In a few weeks we are going to be rich. We will own the woman. And the best part is there will be no trace of us anywhere. And I do mean anywhere."

The intensity in his eyes unnerved Josie.

She cast a probing glance his way as if she'd analyzed the situation, wasn't sure he was right, but hoped he was. Then she changed the subject. "I'm hungry. Can we pick up Thai tonight?"

"Sure, sweetie," Steve grinned. "Which one of these new cards shall we use?"

Chapter 8

In the backwoods of Northbrook, the village's small industrial zone nestled in a mostly residential North Shore neighborhood. Unlike the staid brick colonials and huge showy McMansions on main streets, buildings in the industrial area looked like they'd been slapped together overnight. One story, two at the most, the occasional Quonset hut, and parking lots occupied streets named Anthony and Maria, named after the developer's children. Ellie and Rachel drove up to one of those buildings the next morning.

Inside the glass entrance door, an arrow pointed them down the hall to Suite 105, where an interior door marked with black reflective tape announced they were at the offices of Zach Dolan & Associates.

"Who is this guy?" Rachel asked.

"He's a hacker," Ellie said. She rang the buzzer. A deep bark that had to belong to a large dog replied. The bark was quickly muffled, and a door inside closed. "That was one of his 'Associates.'"

Rachel opened her mouth, about to say something when the door was unlocked and released.

Ellie stared. "Zach? Is that you?"

"The one and only." He grinned. "Great to see you, Ellie."

"Oh my God. You look fabulous!"

He beamed. Almost six feet, Zach had once been a roly-poly guy with dark eyes and beard that matched long tech-weirdo hair. Now, he was clean-shaven, his hair cut short, and he'd lost at least forty pounds. And, as his sleeveless sweatshirt hinted, he was ripped.

"Someone's been working out," Ellie teased.

"Every day."

"It shows."

Zach glanced over at Rachel. She met his gaze. Neither of them were in a hurry to look away. Finally Zach said, "You must be Rachel. I'm Zach Dolan."

Rachel nodded, seemingly at a loss for words.

"Well, come on in. It's great to meet you." He smiled. "And great to see you too, Ellie."

Ellie didn't mention he'd just repeated himself.

～

Rachel didn't expect her mother's hacker guru to be such a hunk. She'd said he looked like Santa Claus with a dark beard. Boy, was she wrong. With his dark eyes and hair, abs of steel, and a genuine smile, he was irresistible.

She looked around the office, which consisted of one spartan room with four computers against the walls and a conference table surrounded by chairs.

"Are you okay with dogs?" Zach asked.

"Sure. I thought I heard some barks."

"That was Joshua." He opened a door Rachel hadn't noticed, and a large German shepherd bounded out, his tail wagging furiously. He raced over to her and laid his head in her lap. She petted him on his head and scratched his ears. His tail wagged even faster. "Hi, Joshua."

"He's Chief of Surveillance for Zach Dolan & Associates."

Rachel laughed. "Figures."

～

The first thing Zach did after Rachel handed him the flash drive was load it into one of the four computers. Ellie and Rachel pulled up chairs. "Surveillance video can be grainy, jumpy, and barely watchable. Or it can be sharp and distinct," Zach said. "A lot depends on the speed at which the tape was recorded." He tapped on the little white triangle in the center of the screen to advance it. They watched as mottled gray turned black and then a picture appeared.

"Hey, we're in luck! Look at that."

Ellie explained. "The bank's video system must be relatively new and speedy because the picture is sharp and clear."

Rachel studied the video, which showed a wide shot of the lobby. "There's my desk!" she said, pointing to the middle of three desks on the left side of the screen. "Or should I say, my former desk."

Zach swiveled around. "You're not there anymore?"

"I got fired yesterday," she said. "That's why we're here."

"Oh. I didn't realize you were personally involved."

Rachel explained what had happened.

"Well, that sucks," Zach said.

"Tell me about it," she said.

He turned back to the video. "So the woman came in around lunchtime?"

"A little later, about one."

Zach fast-forwarded the tape. "See the time code at the bottom of the screen? We'll go to twelve forty-five and run it from there."

Rachel watched herself at her desk, finishing up some clerical work for one of the Vice-Presidents. It was an out-of-body sensation to see herself from an overhead angle, as if God Himself were looking down from on high. She seemed small and meek.

The woman entered the screen.

"This her?" Zach said.

Rachel leaned forward. "It sure is."

The out-of body-feeling persisted throughout her conversation with the pseudo Pamela Cannon. Then came the phone call. Rachel stood and walked around her desk out of shot. The woman looked around surreptitiously, then crept to Rachel's monitor and sat at her desk. She quickly tapped on a couple of screens and stopped.

"Let's go in close. Maybe we can catch her in the act," Zach said eagerly. His computer was able to home in on the desk and the woman, but they couldn't get a close-up of what was on the screen.

"It wouldn't have worked anyway," Ellie said. "We'd have a scroll line."

"A what?" Rachel asked.

"It's a technical thing," Ellie said. "A band that runs from the top to the bottom of the screen."

Rachel tapped her foot. "What about the woman? So far I haven't seen her face. Is there any way we can?"

At that moment, the woman got up from Rachel's chair, and quickly walked back to her seat in front of Rachel's desk. As she sat, she glanced around in every direction.

"Here!" Zach stopped the tape. The woman looked up towards the video camera, but didn't make direct eye contact with it. "Was the camera hidden?"

"I guess so," Rachel said. "I never noticed it."

"Well that's because you never did anything underhanded," Ellie said. "Look at this."

It did appear as if the woman was looking for a camera but couldn't spot one. Frustration washed over her. It was the first time she didn't seem totally confident. A moment later, Rachel re-entered the frame carrying a manila envelope and sat at her desk. Zach backed up the tape to the image of the woman looking for a camera.

"Gotcha!" he said. He spun around again. "OK. Now what?"

Chapter 9

Pamela Cannon templed her hands on her desk and leaned forward. "Are you sure we did the right thing? I mean, doesn't everyone get hacked these days?"

The office was plush, with thick wall-to-wall beige carpeting, a light oak desk, but there were feminine touches, too. Light colors, mostly beige and lavender walls so pale they seemed almost white, warm gray upholstery, and a vase of fresh flowers on her small conference table.

"You aren't just everyone. And Carefill isn't a mom and pop operation," Devin McDuff, Carefill's Chief of IT and Security, replied. "You've said that the products we sell are the difference between life and death for millions. Our competition would love to get their hands on our formulas. Especially the Project."

He turned to Stan Trollop, Carefill's COO, seated in the chair across from him. "Look. I'm here to give you advice, and my advice is to be proactive. Sure, it may turn out just to be some joker hoping to make a windfall at Best Buy. But the fact they got your Social is troubling."

"In that case we should let our IT people know. Make sure we're protected," Stan said.

Devin nodded. "They're on it. We're meeting at two. Can you clear your schedule, Pamela? You too, Stan."

"If it's really that important..." Pamela said doubtfully

"It is."

"What about the police? Aren't they supposed to be investigating?"

"They claim they ran the woman through facial recognition but came up empty. We could ask them to hand it off to the FBI. Or DHS. I think they'd take a look. But again, there's no proof of a crime or any fraudulent activity. Yet."

"Oh, that's just peachy," Stan said irritably. "More bureaucrats rummaging in our system."

"But we've kept everything related to the Project off the corporate servers," Pamela said. "Even the name." She glanced at both men. "Right?"

"They have your Social Security number. That ups the ante," Devin replied.

Pamela felt a sudden chill.

"If they're good, they can hack into your personal email, cell calls, and tablet. And we have been communicating about the Project privately."

She lifted a hand and rubbed her forehead. "So all those prognosticators are right."

"About what?" Devin asked.

"That there really is no more privacy. If this is what it's like to do business today—what do the kids say—it sucks."

Devin shrugged.

"Well, there is some good news," Stan offered. "R&D says they're ready for clinical trials. Expect red tape and delays, but at least we're moving in the right direction."

"What's the chance it will leak to the media?" Pamela asked.

"It will. It might have already, if this 'intrusion' turns out to be what we discussed," Devin said.

"This just gets better and better. I think we ought to prepare for damage control. There's a lot at stake."

"Well," Devin paused. "There are companies, like Kroll and Garda who can consult with us. Give us a crisis plan for communications as well as an actual lockdown. We might want to contact one of them."

"But then the pool of potential leakers widens."

"That's true," he said.

"Christ. We're damned if we do and damned if we don't."

"That's about right. Let's see what IT says. Meanwhile, you've changed all your accounts at the bank? Put a credit freeze on your credit cards?" Devin asked.

She nodded.

"Deleted your social media accounts?"

"Of course. The only one I had was Facebook. And that was just for messaging Laurie."

"Does your daughter know what happened?" Stan asked.

Pamela shook her head. "I'll tell her the next time I visit." She smiled ruefully. "It should be all over by then."

Devin cleared his throat and changed the subject. "You should know we're negotiating with Google to archive all your personal background files, although if someone is stalking you, they may already have what they need."

"Would that include Laurie's profile and data?"

"Most likely."

"That's unacceptable. She has absolutely nothing to do with this." For the first time Pamela's eyes turned steely and her body went rigid. "We have to stop this. I will not allow anyone to go after my daughter."

Neither man replied. Pamela suspected they didn't want to tell her there was no way to avoid it.

She stared at the executives. "This is insane. They have all the advantages. I'm vulnerable to extortion, blackmail, whatever they want, and you're telling me I have to lie back, open my legs, and enjoy it."

"Not entirely. If we go through with—"

She cut him off. "Stop. You're saying even if we protect ourselves, tighten our security, and make a crisis plan, there's still a better than even chance they'll hit me again. Bottom line: I'm naked. So is my daughter. And so is Carefill."

When neither man replied, she repeated, "This is insane."

Chapter 10

Spring, the type of spring where you no longer need a jacket or socks, isn't a sure thing in Chicago until the middle of May. As an ambitious young woman, Rachel had limited her carefree springtime adventures to weekends. Now, though, she didn't have a job, so she was free to enjoy the season any day of the week.

Except that didn't happen. At least, for a while. When Zach asked what they wanted him to do, her mother, Ellie, replied without missing a beat, "Facial recognition."

Zach swiveled around, crossing his arms. "You're assuming I have a database of faces. Or access to one."

"You don't?" Ellie cocked her head, as if she already knew the answer.

"As a matter of fact, I just signed an agreement with some folks that do."

Her mother pointed a finger at him. "I knew it."

Zach pretended to be offended and turned to Rachel. "Some people have sky high expectations, don't they?"

Rachel laughed. "Tell me about it."

"What... expectations or facial recognition?" he asked

"Both."

"Hey, if you want to hang around, I can show you the basics." He turned to Ellie. "I'll give Rachel a ride home later."

Ellie looked from Zach to Rachel. "Sure," she said a little too casually, it seemed to Rachel. "Let me know if you find anything." She sailed out of the office without a backward glance.

～

"Later" turned out to be almost dinnertime. First, Zach showed Rachel how the AI software worked, and they uploaded the shot of the woman in the bank to the database. "It's going to take a few hours, at least, for the software to run through all the possible matches," Zach said.

"That's okay."

"So, let's take Joshua for a walk at the dog park while we're waiting. The one we go to is in Deerfield."

"Great."

Joshua seemed to know where they were going, and as they drove north and west, he grew excited. He was pawing and snuffling at the windows by the time they parked. Zach let him off the leash and the dog, his tail wagging as fast as a windshield wiper in a downpour, bounded down the path to smell and pee and bark.

"You're not afraid he'll run away or get in a dog fight?"

"There's no place to run. It's fenced in but you can't see the chicken wire from here. As for fights, Joshua's a big dog. An alpha male. Most dogs would rather have him on their side."

Rachel shaded her eyes with her hand. She could barely see Joshua anymore, but Zach didn't seem concerned. They walked the path behind him. "So," she said, "tell me about being a hacker."

"How much time do you have?"

She shrugged. "Plenty, these days."

"Okay. Basically, I switched sides."

"How come?"

"I used to hack into systems. In fact, I got pretty good at it. Then, my brother helped me get a job working for The Man, doing the same thing. Once I realized I could do what I love and be on the right side of the law, well, it didn't take a rocket scientist to figure out where I should be."

"What is it you love about hacking?"

"Discovering the secrets. Everyone and every organization has them. Maybe they know what those secrets are, maybe they don't. I love looking for them. They're like pieces of a puzzle, and there's nothing more satisfying than putting those pieces together so we can catch bad guys who try to profit from them."

Rachel brightened. "That's exactly what I thought when I joined the police academy," she said. "I really wanted to catch bad guys and make sure what happened to me *never* happened to anyone else. But I couldn't handle the violence. Every time I went to target practice or worked with explosives, I freaked out."

"Your mother told me what happened to you. I'm so sorry you went through that."

"Mom keeps telling me everything will click at some point, and that I'll know what I was put on this earth for." She paused. "I keep waiting for that to happen."

"For the record, I think your mom is right." He smiled. "It happened to me."

Rachel snapped her finger. "So, just like that, you went to work?"

He shook his head. "First, I had to get certified, which doesn't mean a whole lot, but corporations today demand hackers have certifications. It's one of the only ways to weed out guys they have doubts about. CEH and OSCP are the big ones."

Mouth open, Joshua bounded back up, sniffed Zach and Rachel, then ran away again.

"Do we need to follow him?"

Zach looked amused. "Nope. He just wants to know we're still here. He'll be back.

So, where was I?"

"Certification."

"Right. So with hackers, it used to be pretty simple. You hacked. You either got caught, or you didn't. But now, there are different hacker types. Specialization, you know," he cracked. "Most people talk about white hats, which is me, and black hats which are the bad guys. But there are red hat hackers too."

"What are they?"

He laughed. "They're kind of like the Eagle Scouts of hacking. I think of them as white hackers with an attitude. Like white hats, red hats attack black hats or protect against them. But they are ruthless bastards. They'll keep on destroying the black hats after they've penetrated their systems, so thoroughly that the bad guys sometimes need to replace their own systems."

"That seems harsh."

"Not really. If someone tries to cripple your system, and you cripple theirs back, they'd probably think twice before going after you again, wouldn't they?"

"I guess."

"And if the black hat is from a country that isn't a pal of ours, well, you might say the red hat is a hero, right?"

"Why do I have the feeling you wouldn't mind being a red hat?"

"People grow up. Even me."

By the time they arrived back at Zach's office with a tired dog, sandwiches, and pop, the facial recognition program had completed its run without finding a match.

"That's not good," Rachel ventured.

"Doesn't mean much. They update it all the time with new faces."

"Where do they get them?"

"Both public and private sources. So, I'll keep checking." He tossed her a book. "Here, read this. You can give it back to me when you're done."

Rachel turned the book over to read the title, *I Created The Melissa Virus,* by David Lee Smith. "Who's he?"

"You'll find out. It's a good place to start."

When he dropped her off at her apartment, Zach hesitated. Then he leaned over and kissed her. Rachel kissed him back. His after-shave, a clean fresh scent with an undertone of sandalwood, smelled sexy. After he left, she searched for the right word to describe how she felt about Zach. He was different than the other men she'd dated. Only a few years older, it wasn't that he was more mature. Or smart. Both of which he was. She was attracted to him, no question. But what was it that made her want to see him again? She thought about it. Finally, she figured it out. With Zach she felt secure.

Chapter 11

Two weeks later, Steve dropped Josie off at O'Hare in the afternoon. Armed with a new driver's license under the name of Pamela Cannon, a plane ticket to Miami, and several new credit cards all in Cannon's name, she sailed through security and spent the time before her flight at the airline's VIP lounge with a dry martini and peanuts. She took her seat in First Class and settled down with the newest D.C. tell-all by a prominent journalist. A few minutes after take-off, she dozed off.

When the plane landed three hours later, she was met in baggage claim by a uniformed chauffer with a printed sign that said, "Pamela Cannon." She greeted him regally and told him what her luggage looked like, then waited for him to retrieve it.

He drove her to The Four Winds on Miami Beach, an ultra-luxurious hotel where she had reserved a suite with a view of the ocean. She checked in, waited for the bell cap to bring her suitcase, and tipped him ten. Then she unpacked and changed her clothes.

Josie was still a looker, even in her forties, and she made sure she was at her most attractive. White capri pants, a black silk top and sandals. She freed her blond streaked hair, wore it down, and carefully applied her make-up.

An hour later she descended from the suite to the bar. This wasn't the typical Chicago tavern she was used to. This bar twinkled with Italian lights, which were reflected in a huge mirror in back. A tuxedoed bartender poured drinks, and soft music floated out of hidden speakers. Josie took a seat at a small table and ordered a dry martini and a shrimp ceviche appetizer.

Within a few minutes, a man at the bar swung around and stared at her. For a while she pretended not to notice him, but when she did, she shot him a smile. He promptly slid off his stool and came over to her table.

"May I join you?" he asked.

"Nice work, Donny," she replied. He was in an expensive sports jacket, slacks, white shirt, and penny loafers. Recalling their drink when he was in sweats, she smiled. "You clean up well." To be honest, he wasn't bad looking, except for a pockmarked face that must have caused him teenage anguish when he was young.

"So, why am I here?" he asked.

"You wanted to meet my partner. We decided you were right. So you're going to meet him later. And, of course, we thought you'd like to watch us do a dry run." She remembered he liked booze. "How about we order another round? Just remember, tonight I'm Pamela. Got it?"

He nodded. They drank and chatted as if they were strangers who'd met unexpectedly.

After about an hour, she asked if he'd like to get something to eat, and they moved to a table in the hotel's restaurant. Josie found dinner tedious, especially when Don started to come onto her.

"Would you be doing this with the real Pamela Cannon?" she asked icily.

"Are you shitting me?"

"Then, don't do it with me."

Don looked around the dining room. "When is your partner gonna get here?"

"Soon." She smiled patiently.

They finished their entrees: hers mahi-mahi, his a steak.

Although they skipped dessert, she was fed up with his "You know, you're a pretty hot looking babe" and "Why don't you give me your room key?" When he tried to take her hand, she pulled away.

"What? Are you married?" Don asked.

"You are," she countered.

"How do you know?"

"I told you. You're not dealing with amateurs, Don. We do our homework. Plus you're my client. You know what they say about shitting where you eat."

"So that means—"

"I'm off limits." She smiled again.

"Hey, maybe I should call you Pammy. That's what her husband called her. Before he died."

She finished the wine they'd ordered, a nice rosé, and cocked her head. "So, Don. We never got into details. Why did she ax you?"

He flushed from the neck up. Then he waved a hand. "I don't want to get into it."

"A little late for that. You're already working for me. Let me guess. She figured out you were embezzling money from the payroll."

"Something like that. But I wasn't. Not really."

"What does that mean? Either you were, or you weren't."

"I was just—balancing things here and there. Like in *Ocean's Eleven*. Hey. I gave that company over twenty years of my life."

"Some nerve! She fired you just because you stole money from the company?" Josie checked her iPhone. "Hey, how about we go for a walk on the beach? Let our dinners settle?"

"Is your partner out there?"

"Maybe. Why do you care so much? Don't trust a woman to do the job?"

"I do trust you. I just want to see the guy I gave fifty grand to." He paid for their dinners, and they walked through a glass door that led directly to the beach. Dark now and quieter than the restaurant, the shadows on the beach cloaked everything in a pool of black. They strolled to the end of the hotel property. A grove of palm and other tropical-looking trees with gnarled branches and thick green foliage marked the edge of the Four Winds property. Josie led Don into the copse. When they were far enough in so they weren't visible to anyone walking by, she stopped. They heard a whistle.

"What's that?" Don asked.

Josie shrugged. "A bird, probably." She faced him, and slipped her arms around Don's neck. "Ok. True confession. I've been waiting to do this all night," she said in a sultry whisper.

"Really? Then what was all that—" She quieted him by kissing him. She kissed him repeatedly, on his lips, his cheeks, and his neck, making sure he was becoming more aroused with each move. When his hands went from the small of her back to her breasts, he moaned.

"Oh, Pammy. You taste delicious."

"Ummm," Josie cooed. "I'm glad you think so." She was surprised he'd called her Pammy. That explained a lot.

Those were the last words Donald Fields heard. Suddenly a knife appeared in Josie's field of vision. She watched as a man drew it back, clasped his other hand over Fields' mouth, and stabbed Fields on the side of his neck. The man pulled the knife out, and stabbed him again somewhere in his back. Blood spurted from his carotid. Josie staggered back, momentarily frozen.

Still, she had to give it to Fields; he was silent as he arched back, a look of sudden surprise on his face. As he collapsed, Steve caught him and eased him down onto the ground.

"Nicely done, Josie. We make a good team."

Chapter 12

Pamela Cannon was proud that she could still do a clean dive. She'd been on the swim team in college, and although the team never won any major competitions, she'd kept up the practice of swimming laps. Other people might think laps were boring, but they simultaneously calmed and energized her, washing away minutiae from her mind.

She turned her head. Breathed in. Stroked and exhaled. Turned her head, breathed in, and repeated the process. A simple focus on form occupied the front part of her brain... what was the correct term? Pre-frontal cortex. Yes. The irony was that all sorts of thoughts and impulses might be percolating in other parts of her brain, but she wasn't aware of them. All she knew was that when she emerged from the pool after two-thirds of a mile, the knots of daily stress had eased, and she felt prepared to face the rest of her day. Or night.

Sometime during her swim that evening, she became aware that someone had entered the pool area on the top floor of her Gold Coast condo building. She didn't break stride or look up, but her peripheral vision picked up the presence of a woman. Not a swimmer. A watcher. As long as the voyeur didn't bother her, they could watch as long as they wanted. Although why someone would want to lurk in an uncomfortably overheated, chlorine-smelling atmosphere was puzzling.

Forty minutes later, she swam to the shallow end and using her shoulders, lifted herself out of the pool. Stripping off her goggles, she glanced over to the side of the pool. The woman was gone.

Pamela grabbed her towel and proceeded to the dressing room. Since she was just going downstairs to her condo, she threw her swimsuit into a locker, put on some sweats, wrapped her hair in a towel, and went out to punch the elevator button. The elevator chirped and the door slid open. She stepped in.

Five minutes later, as Pamela seasoned a small filet and plopped it onto her terrace grill, her doorbell rang. Must be someone in the building. Everyone from the outside was vetted by the doorman, a former cop.

"Who's there, please?" she asked and peered through the tiny magnifying glass. It was the woman from the pool with two men.

"Police, ma'am. We'd like a word with you."

The trim African-American, thirty-ish woman, introduced herself. "I'm Lieutenant Detective Hartley and these men are Sergeant Connelly and Officer Ludlum."

"Sorry, I just got out of the pool." She looked at Hartley. "Could I see some ID please?"

After Hartley showed Pamela her badge, Pamela asked, "Was that you watching me upstairs?"

"Yes, ma'am."

"I see." She didn't, but she led them into her living room. "Please sit down. Do you have some news for me?"

Hartley frowned. "News? I don't understand."

"About the fraud."

"What fraud?"

"The theft of my Social Security number."

"Your social was stolen?" Hartley asked.

Pamela started to run a hand through her hair but she reached the towel instead. Irritated, she dropped her hand. "You're not here about the identity theft that was perpetrated on me? I filed a police report. Hold on. I'll find a copy."

"Ma'am. I'm not here about any fraud orr identity theft. We're here because a man was killed on Miami Beach five days ago, on April twelfth."

"I'm sorry to hear that, but what does that have to do with me?"

"The victim had been an employee of Carefill. His name was Donald Fields."

Pamela winced, squeezed her eyes shut, and took in a breath. When she opened her eyes, Hartley said,

"What is it, Ms. Cannon?"

"He was the Director of Payroll. I fired him a month ago."

"Ma'am, we have reason to think you were involved in his murder."

Chapter 13

Dr. Richard Hookie, or Hook, as his Vietnam buddies called him, hunched over his desk in his office at Stone Mountain Medical Center in Atlanta, Georgia. He was reading a paper from one of the medical students and hating every minute of it. At seventy-four he was an M.D. with a PhD in genetics and held a prestigious position doing research at the medical center. He occasionally taught classes in genetics and biology for second year med students but spent most of his time in the lab. One of the full-time professors passed student papers to him if he wanted a second opinion about them.

An M.D. colleague did, and as Hook read the paper, he realized why. The student had plagiarized most of his content. It wasn't even a clever attempt; the student had compared Alzheimer's to other types of dementia, and it looked like he'd copied his content verbatim from Wikipedia and PublicDoc.com. The professor conveniently included printouts of the Turn-It-In report.

Hook sighed, crossed out every page in the student's paper with red marker, and wrote a huge "F" across the top. When would these kids realize that being in his seventies didn't mean he was mentally deficient? Or couldn't surf the net? Especially when it came to

Alzheimer's. His best friend in Vietnam had been diagnosed with early onset Alzheimer's twenty-five years after serving in 'Nam, and part of Hook's initial interest was selfish; he wanted to make sure nobody else in his buddy's family would inherit the disease.

At first, his hunch was that it was related to Agent Orange or other toxins that spewed down over the battlefields. But after months of research, he had no proof and grew frustrated. Eventually, he'd moved on.

His intercom buzzed. His secretary said, "Dr. Hook, it's David Stearns from Homeland Security."

Although he was bald on the top of his head, Hook tugged on his ponytail of silvery gray, which held the sides and back of his hair. He rose from his desk and stretched out his lanky body, especially his right leg, which he favored with a limp. "Put him through, Donna."

"Yes sir."

"Hook?"

He cleared his throat. "How you doing, David?"

"As well as can be expected," the Homeland Security official replied.

"Guess that new virus is keeping you busy."

"You don't know the half of it." Stearns groaned. "But actually, that's not why I'm calling."

Hook straightened and pushed the receiver closer to his ear. "Oh?"

"I have some questions for you," the Homeland Security official said.

Chapter 14

Pamela Cannon sat in a small, windowless room with white walls deep in the bowels of the Chicago Police Precinct just south of Division on Larrabee. A lawyer, Rich Summers, sat beside her with a legal pad and fountain pen. Across from them was Lieutenant Gina Hartley, the officer who'd come to her condo an hour earlier. Next to her was a man, clearly Hartley's superior. A crusty sixtyish man with a lined face and a belly that obscured his belt, he was casually dressed in jeans and a sweatshirt. His badge was pinned to his sweatshirt. He introduced himself as Commander Mike Green.

"Appreciate you coming down this evening, Ms. Cannon."

Pamela, in beige linen pants and a brown sweater, nodded. "Of course, Commander. I want to get this sorted out as much as you."

"Ms. Cannon has nothing to hide, Commander Green," Summers cut in.

Cannon flashed Summers a sidelong glance. She wasn't a big fan of the attorney. He reminded her of Stephen Mnuchin, Donald Trump's Secretary of the Treasury. A weasel, she thought. Swarmy. But her personal attorney was on vacation, and she was stuck with Summers, apparently the on-call attorney for after-hours emergencies.

"In fact, we welcome your involvement," Summers said with a plastic smile.

Pamela wanted to roll her eyes but managed not to.

Commander Green turned to her. "So what you're telling us is that someone stole your identity a few weeks ago."

"That's correct, Commander," Cannon answered. "A woman impersonated me at one of the banks I use and managed to get my Social Security number. I filed a police report the next day, and frankly, I was told by my attorney—not Mr. Summers—that the police report was key. Without it the police really wouldn't be able to do much. I never expected anything like this to happen."

The Commander nodded. "So your position is that you had nothing to do with the murder in Florida?"

Summers cut in. "Of course she didn't. She's the CEO of a Fortune 500 company."

"Right," the Commander said. "And my name is Abraham Lincoln."

Cannon spread her hands. "Sir, I have no idea what happened in Florida. I was concerned with identity theft. The first time I heard about a murder was when your officer came to my condo. I'm shocked. And saddened. But I had nothing to do with it."

"Let's talk about the identity theft for a minute," the Commander said. "You filed a police report, but you didn't do anything after the breach of your Social?"

"We were waiting for you—I mean, whoever would be investigating the report—to get back to me."

The commander nodded and leaned back in his chair. His hands disappeared below the table. She could see him hitch his belt up over his belly.

"So you didn't do anything?"

"That's not the case. I transferred the money to a new account. And we tightened security measures at Carefill."

"Was the new account at the same bank?"

"Yes."

Hartley, who sat next to Green, pushed a piece of paper toward him.

"And yet an account in your name was opened at Chase on the same day you claimed you moved your funds to a new account."

"I don't know anything about that. I don't bank there."

"Did you check the balance of the funds you transferred? Was any money missing?"

Cannon felt her cheeks get hot. "I—I'm embarrassed to tell you I did not. I have—"

Summers cut in again. "As you know, Ms. Cannon is CEO of Carefill, Incorporated. She works fifteen, sixteen hours a day. She has a personal assistant who handles deposits and withdrawals for her personal issues."

Hartley threw Summers a skeptical frown, but Commander Green's expression remained neutral. "So you're saying you had no knowledge that a new bank account was opened in your name?"

"That's correct," Cannon rubbed one wrist with her other hand. Her arthritic wrist throbbed. "I—I can see now that I should have paid more attention."

"Commander," Summers said, "This is clearly a fraudulent situation. The timing is too coincidental to the theft of her social."

Green turned to Hartley. "Do we know who got the police report and whether they followed up?"

"I checked, sir. It was forwarded to Lieutenant Dave Case down in Fraud. He hasn't returned my call."

Green folded his arms. He didn't look pleased.

"Sir," Hartley said, "I will personally retrieve the report and do what I can."

"Good." He turned to Cannon and Summers. "Let's get back to the crime in Florida. Lieutenant Hartley has some questions for you." He nodded for her to go ahead.

"Ms. Cannon, how long did you know Donald Fields?"

"I met him when he was promoted to Director of Payroll six years ago."

"Why did you fire him?"

"My IT people discovered he'd been embezzling from Carefill over the past eighteen months."

"How much did he take?"

"It was about fifty thousand dollars. In small increments. He thought he was being careful. At least, that's what he told Devin when he confronted him."

"Devin?

"Devin McDuff, Director of IT."

"Ms. Cannon, I checked our records as well as a national data base, but you never filed a police report."

"That's correct. He claimed his mother had Alzheimer's and he needed the money for her care."

"Was that the truth?"

"It was. We checked. I—he made restitution for every penny, but I couldn't trust him, so I let him go. At the time, I thought that was sufficient."

"I see." Hartley's voice was expressionless. Pamela suspected Hartley didn't believe her. Then again, that was a police officer's job. Hartley glanced at her notes, shuffled some paper, looked up. "Ms. Cannon, did you take an Amm's limo to O'Hare on April 12 at 1:25 PM?"

Pamela opened her daybook. Unlike most executives, she kept her calendar on a black day-by-day notebook. What if her computer didn't work? Or there was a power failure? Better safe than sorry. She opened it to April 12. "No, Lieutenant. I was here in Chicago."

Hartley's eyebrows shot sky high. "Is there someone who can vouch for you?"

Cannon smiled. "Anyone on my staff. You are welcome to call them."

"Did you board United Flight #509 to Miami on a first class ticket?"

"No again, Lieutenant."

"Did you take a limo from the Miami airport to the Four Winds hotel on Miami Beach?"

Cannon shook her head.

"Please say yes or no."

"No."

"Did you order drinks from the Four Winds bar the evening of April 12?"

"I did not."

"Dinner from the hotel restaurant?"

"No, Lieutenant."

Hartley held up a paper. "Miami Police have your name, address, credit cards, even your Social Security number."

Summers replied. "May I have a copy of that report? So we can analyze the alleged sightings and records?"

Cannon decided Summers wasn't so bad after all. He was doing a good job protecting her. Still, the police couldn't possibly believe she was a killer, could they?

Hartley and Green exchanged frustrated glances. Then Green said, "That would be helpful. If what you say is true, we have a hell of a mess on our hands. I might ask the FBI to step in. They have experts and resources we don't."

Cannon said, "I appreciate that, Commander. You're right about it being a mess. Never in my life did I expect to have my identity stolen. And to be accused of murder? That's just unbelievable. A nightmare. I hope no one is trying—"

Summers glared at her. Cannon stopped in mid-sentence.

"What were you going to say?" Commander Green asked.

Cannon looked at Summers, and then back at the Commander. She decided to proceed. "If it's just me they're after, I will deal with that. But what if their real target is Carefill?"

No one answered.

Chapter 15

Pamela was typically a sound sleeper, but when she woke up her sheets and blanket were bunched up around her feet, and two of her four pillows were on the floor. She showered and dressed and was at her desk at Carefill's headquarters in the Loop before seven. Unlike other behemoth Chicago healthcare companies such as Abbott and Baxter, Carefill's headquarters were still in the Loop rather than the suburbs, although, admittedly, the operating costs of doing so were becoming burdensome.

She made a few calls to Carefill's overseas operations and made a list of the issues raised and action plans brainstormed. Reluctantly, she agreed to fly to Paris for a meeting the next day. Her assistant, Kelly, wouldn't be in until eight. Pamela impatiently tapped her pen on her desk. She recalled doing that in middle school. She was way ahead of the other students in algebra and would solve an equation sooner than anyone else. She'd tap her pencil on her desk while she waited, pretending she was Ringo Starr playing an original riff. The other kids hated her for that, and the teacher made her stop. Now, she almost smiled. No one would stop her now.

Finally, Kelly arrived and brought in Pamela's skinny vanilla latte, one of the few indulgences she permitted herself. This morning, though, the latte tasted like chalk.

"Kelly, I need to see my statements from Midwest Mutual right away. Both last month's and the current one. On paper. And I need to fly to Paris tonight. Oh, and as long as I'm nearby, get me to Brussels. I'll have dinner with Laurie."

Kelly withdrew and a few moments later Pamela heard the clunk of printers. The assistant returned with two sets of papers.

"Thanks," Pamela smiled. "And thanks for the latte."

"Is something wrong?" Kelly asked. She and Kelly had become closer ever since Laurie moved to Brussels. Kelly was about Laurie's age, early thirties.

Pamela scanned both documents. "Did you move thirty thousand out of one of the Midwest Mutual accounts?"

Kelly shook her head. "It's been a quiet month. Except for the usual bills which I paid, nothing."

"You're sure?"

"Absolutely. If you want, I'll show you the spreadsheets." When Pamela handed over her personal accounts for Kelly to administer, she and Kelly agreed that whenever Pamela asked her to deposit or write a check above a thousand dollars, Kelly would enter it on a spreadsheet. There was a spreadsheet for each account: three at Midwest Mutual, and two others at RBC.

"Would you check the other Midwest Mutual accounts?"

"Sure." A moment later, a new email chirped on Pamela's desktop. The spreadsheets were attached.

Kelly came back into the office. "I have your reservation for Paris. First class, leaves at seven thirty tonight."

Pamela looked up from the spreadsheets. "We have a problem. Between the three accounts, over one hundred thousand dollars has been withdrawn."

Kelly's eyes widened. "That can't be right."

"Someone hacked into my accounts," Pamela said angrily. "It's got to be the woman who got hold of my Social."

"Identity theft? What should I do?" Kelly asked.

Pamela's face smoothed out. "Close those accounts right away. We'll move them."

~

By late afternoon, Pamela had closed her three Midwest Mutual accounts and transferred them to another bank. She declined to take two phone calls from officers of Midwest Mutual. They'd know why she closed the accounts. She called Stan and told him about the upcoming Paris meeting.

"You want me to go in your place?"

"Normally, I would. But I thought I'd swing by and visit Laurie while I'm there."

"Good idea."

She let him know about the withdrawals from her Midwest Mutual bank accounts. "Please tell Devin to coordinate with the bank's Fraud Department. Make sure they turn everything over to Chicago PD. I'll leave him a VM, but I'd like his advice. I'm feeling quite out of balance, and I need stability, not a nasty surprise every time I turn around."

She went home early to pack for Paris and Brussels, figuring she'd be gone for three days top, excluding travel. She made herself a sandwich, drank a glass of wine, and Ubered to the airport. She liked the simplicity of an Uber. One didn't always need a limo.

Once she was through security, she went to the United Club Lounge, grabbed another glass of wine, and started to read her emails. She was in the middle of a lengthy response to a supplier in Malaysia when she heard, "Ms. Cannon, could you please come to the ticket agent desk?"

Now what? She sighed, closed her laptop, and took the stairs down where a uniformed ticket agent behind the counter was waiting.

"I'm Pamela Cannon," she said to the agent, a middle-aged woman who looked almost as tired as Pamela felt.

"Ms. Cannon, there is an issue with your passport."

"Excuse me?"

"As you may know, the airline screens all passengers' IDs and passports ahead of boarding, especially with First Class passengers."

Pamela stiffened. This was not going to be good news. "And?"

"When we ran yours, another passport number came up. It's different from yours."

"What are you talking about? That's impossible. I travel internationally all the time."

"Apparently, there is a second passport with your name, address, and personal information, but the photo is not you. Neither is the number."

"Which means?"

The ticket agent bit her lip. "I can't say. All I was told is that under the circumstances, with two purported passports for you, Homeland Security cannot authorize your travel. You should take it up with them."

"But I'm on my way to an important meeting in Paris."

"I'm so sorry, ma'am. There's nothing I can do."

Pamela shook her head. "I don't understand this at all." She did, of course, but she hoped the woman would give her more information if she played dumb.

The ticket agent let out a breath. "I'm not supposed to say anything, Ms. Cannon, but it could be identity theft." She flipped up her hands. "But you didn't hear that from me."

"Wait a minute. I thought there were all sorts of security measures on the passport itself that prevented it from being duplicated."

"I can't advise you on that, Ma'am. Again, I understand your frustration. I'm very sorry."

Pamela was fuming. She went back upstairs, grabbed her briefcase, and made a phone call. This time she took a limo home.

Chapter 16

After the murder Josie and Steve fled from the beach and hurried inside the Four Winds to the elevators. Josie was close to panic. "Oh god, oh god."

Steve took her arm and whispered. "Be quiet. We'll talk upstairs." They stepped into the elevator, but Josie was still whimpering. Steve quickly located the camera inside and wrapped his arms around her, giving the camera his back. "Shh..." he kissed her. "Quiet." He kissed her again.

Finally, when they were inside her suite, she collapsed onto the sofa. "I've never seen someone murdered before. I've never even seen someone die."

"I told you to prepare yourself. This wasn't going to be a picnic."

"I know, I know..." she sniffed, "but.. it was awful. All that blood, and it was warm. How could you, Steve?"

"We didn't have a choice. You'll see. We're going to be fine. I have a plan. I told you."

"Yes, but it was just a plan before. Words, like a TV show or a book. I never thought about actually being part of it."

"Like I said, it had to be done."

"Did it really?" She looked at him, tears still welling in her eyes.

Steve went to her, sat, and put his arms around her. His shirt and hands smelled coppery, almost metallic. Like Fields' blood.

"Look," he said. "He was an easy mark. We needed the money. He could have identified us. Now we take the rest of the money from her account and sail down to Mexico until things calm down." He looked around the room. "Get your things together, and we'll get out of here. You gave them the new AmEx card when you checked in, right?"

"How can you think about that?"

"I have to. You did that, right?"

"I did."

"Good. That will lead the cops straight to Cannon once they discover the body. Now. Get yourself together and let's go. Time is not our friend."

Josie wiped the tears from her cheeks and threw the few items she'd unpacked back into her carry-on.

"You okay?"

She shrugged.

Steve and Josie took an Uber under assumed names to a twenty-four hour Avis outlet and rented a green Honda with a forged driver's license and credit card. It took them four hours to drive north to Fort Lauderdale, where they picked up Alligator Alley to Naples, then north again to Fort Myers, and finally to Captiva Island. Josie dozed for much of the ride.

The dawn sky was streaked with gold-tinged pink clouds by the time they arrived. The small resort sat on the Bay side of the island. It was past high season, and most of the snowbirds and vacationers were gone, so they were able to get a room. As soon as they walked in, Steve fired up his laptop.

"Shit."

"What's wrong?" Josie wrapped her arms around herself. Her anxiety had been under control during the trip, but now it flared again.

"She knows we've been hacking her accounts," Steve said. "She closed all three of them. They're gone."

"Does she know it's us?"

Steve didn't answer. Despite the potential danger that Cannon might have arranged for someone to electronically watch and track anyone trying to access her now closed accounts, his pulse sped up. They were beginning a cat-and-mouse game. He would hack into her new accounts. He had figured she'd moved them to National Trust. Carefill had a relationship with the bank. Steve would need more finesse to get in. National's security was pretty tight.

He could do it, but there were three problems. The first was that he'd have to drain everything in the account that contained Cannon's stolen money and transfer it in a hurry to yet another new account at a new bank. The second problem was that Cannon now knew someone was after her, and while he himself operated with layers of security, masking his tracks with VPNs and hacking into at least three other domains before he took any action, nothing in cyberspace was a lock. The third problem was that he was running out of time. At least Fields was out of the way.

"Steve, I'm talking to you."

"What? I'm sorry, babe. Why don't you go get some breakfast? This place is supposed to serve the best on the island."

"I don't give a damn about breakfast. I want to know if we're in danger," Josie said.

"We're fine. But don't get too comfortable. We won't be here long."

The next day Josie woke up and stretched like a cat. Time had improved her mood. "Well, it's been a couple of days and nothing's happened. Maybe we *can* pull this off."

Steve didn't reply.

"Hey, I'm hungry. Let's get some food."

Steve looked up from the laptop. "Why don't you get something, then go to the beach? I'll come down when I'm finished."

"How long will you be?" she asked.

"An hour or so."

"Okay. Good thing I packed a suit." She pulled out a bikini, went into the bathroom and emerged a minute later with the black and white suit on her body.

"Oh my God, you look delicious."

Josie smiled.

"Come here."

She sauntered over, swinging her hips from side to side. Steve stood up, slipped his arms around her, and carried her over to the bed.

Chapter 17

It was almost eleven o'clock by the time Josie finished breakfast and walked to the stretch of white sand owned by the resort. The place boasted that its beach, unlike others on Sanibel and Captiva, was pure sand rather than the mix of sand and shells for which the islands were known. At one end of the strip of beach was a bar. The bartender doubled as the guy who set up umbrellas and loungers. Josie asked him to set up a lounger for her, then ordered a mai tai. She lay down on the lounger and sipped her drink, trying to forget about the events of the past twenty-four hours.

The Gulf water, bright blue with tiny whitecaps on the waves, was choppy. Having had almost three months to warm up, it wouldn't be cold. When she finished her drink, she got up and wandered to the edge of the water. She walked into the Gulf until she was waist deep and started to breaststroke parallel to the shore. The water felt refreshing, but the undertow kicked more than she'd expected. A few minutes later, she was ready to come out. She picked her way back to the edge of the shore, but she wasn't wearing sunglasses, and as she emerged from the water, she went temporarily sun blind.

She could hear, however, and the sudden "spit-spit" of bullets from a high-powered rifle zipped past her and then slammed into her chest. Within seconds, Josie was down, her black and white bikini now saturated with red.

Steve heard the sirens from his room and stopped working. He went to his window and peeked out. A firetruck, ambulance, and police car had converged on the beach, and a crowd was forming to one side. Fear rippled through his gut.

He picked up the phone in their room and called down to the front desk.

"Front desk," an excited male voice said.

"What's going on?" Steve asked.

"Not sure yet. They're saying someone was shot and killed on the beach."

Nausea climbed up Steve's throat, making it difficult for him to speak. "Who—what happened?"

"All I know is it was a woman."

Steve didn't say anything. "Do you know who?"

"Can't talk right now. The cops are coming in." The line disconnected.

Steve shut down his laptop and hurriedly packed the few things he'd brought. He debated whether to take Josie's things. He shouldn't. She would want them when she got back to the room. He took his laptop and bag down to the Honda, threw them in the trunk, and sauntered over to the beach.

The crowd had grown larger. He couldn't work his way through without attracting attention to himself. Instead, he asked a blowsy woman who was craning her neck what she was seeing.

"They're loading a gurney with the victim's body into the ambulance."

"What does she look like?" he asked, trying to make his voice sound casual.

"I don't know," the woman said. "But she was wearing a black and white bikini."

A burst of panic jolted him. Steve whipped around, raced to the Honda, fired the engine, and sped away.

Chapter 18

Rachel, absorbed in an article about artificial intelligence, hunched over a computer at Zach's office the next morning. She knew nothing about AI, but was trying to learn the basics. Happily, Zach was a patient teacher, and Rachel wrote down her questions to ask when he got back from his workout.

She knew Siri and Alexa were types of AI, albeit primitive when compared to some other applications. The idea that machines could actually learn to think, analyze, and make decisions faster and more thoroughly than humans creeped her out. She remembered reading a Dean Koontz novel years earlier where humans and machines actually fused together and evolved into a new sentient being. The concept still made her shiver.

She was reading about AI applications in finance and banking when another computer in the office dinged. This computer, she knew, was the one that received email alerts they'd set for anything connected to "Pamela Cannon." It dinged every day. Pamela Cannon was one of the country's leading female CEOs, and there was usually something in the business, healthcare, or Chicago press about her, but none of the alerts had anything about her recent identity theft issues.

Until now.

Rachel went to that computer and read the alert. Then she sat down and tapped out the URL. An article from the News-Press in Fort Myers reported that a woman had been shot by a high-powered rifle on Captiva Island, Florida a day earlier. The victim's ID identified her as Pamela Cannon. Two photos accompanied the article. One was a the picture of the beach where "Cannon" was shot; the other was a driver's license photo of the victim. When Rachel saw it, she called Zach.

Thirty minutes later, she and Zach matched the driver's license photo to the video image of the woman at the bank.

"What do we do now?" Rachel asked. She'd been in a state of nervous agitation ever since she read the story. "Shouldn't we call the bank, or better, Carefill? And the police?"

Zach blew out a breath. "If we matched the woman, chances are Chicago police did too."

"Are you sure? You said yourself there was only so much the cops could—or would—do."

"That's true. But there must be other people looking into Cannon's situation. Maybe the FBI. Maybe a private eye. Who knows? At this point, we're not adding anything of value, you know what I mean?"

"You mean because I'm just a fired employee looking to clear her name?"

"To be honest, partly. The FBI's FRS is bound to have caught the match. Anyway, we don't have an official role in this investigation."

Rachel tipped her head to the side. "Yet."

"Really? You sure you want to go there?"

Rachel nodded eagerly, her blond curls bobbing. "Absolutely."

"In that case, we need to give them more than what's in that article." He tapped his foot, as if trying to decide what they should do next. "Tell you what. Feed the DMV image into Google Images.

Search everything carefully. Even if it looks off base. Go down every citation to the end. You'll probably find a bunch of women who resemble the photo. Make a note of their names and save them all. Then, we'll throw everything into the FR database and see what happens."

Rachel grinned. "Aye, aye, Captain."

Zach leaned over and brushed her cheek with his fingers.

"Hey," Rachel said. "No fooling around when we're working. We agreed." But she was smiling.

By noon, Rachel had combed through twenty-four pages of Google Images. Some of the photos that popped up were the real Pamela Cannon, but there were more than a dozen women whose names, and sometimes their photos, surfaced. Zach had warned her that facial recognition software wasn't perfect. There were still bugs to work out in every app. Depending on the criteria used to identify faces, the app could generate false positives or skip true matches.

She shared the results with Zach, and he popped all the faces into the database to compare them to the video of the imposter at the bank. Five of the women came back as potential matches. Plus two new faces that she hadn't seen on Google. One of the two was a police booking photo.

"Check this out," Zach said. "It's from McHenry County." McHenry was just west of Cook County and Chicago.

"Where'd that come from?"

"The database pulls from a lot of public records, including police mugshots."

He tapped on the photo. The police booking report accompanying the photo identified the woman as Jocelyn Warner. She'd been arrested for possession and distribution of meth. The photo looked to be at least ten years old, but when they compared it to the woman in the bank, it was a match. Except for the scowl on Warner's mugshot.

"Oh my God," Rachel cried. "We've got her!"

"Hold on there, babe. We need to double check." Zach compared the new "Pamela Cannon" driver's license photo to the mugshot. A match. Then the mugshot to the bank video again. A match.

"So," Rachel said, "we now know the woman in the bank was a former drug dealer named Jocelyn Warner. And that she was murdered at an island resort. What does that mean? What should we do?"

"Didn't you say your mother had a passing acquaintance with the real Pamela Cannon?"

Rachel nodded.

"I think it's time to give your mom a call."

Chapter 19

The next morning six people sat around a polished oak conference room table on the thirty-fifth floor of Carefill's headquarters: Rachel and Zach, Ellie Foreman, Stan Trollop, Devin McDuff, and Pamela Cannon. Across from Rachel was a window with a view to the southeast. It was a gray, foggy day, and though gauzy bursts of mist shot past the window, she could see the ground. The sight of Chicago's elegant architecture and skyscrapers hugging the beach in the middle of downtown always gave her goosebumps. She was proud to live in a beautiful city where the beach was just feet away from the heart of downtown.

"We're still waiting for the FBI to arrive, correct?" Pamela asked.

"That's right, Pam," Stan said. "I'm not sure everyone knows this, but Chicago PD, with the bank's approval, turned over Pamela's case to the Feds. They're sending over two special agents."

"All right. Does everyone have what they need?" Pamela gestured to a coffee pot and tray of fruit and pastries. "Ellie," she added, "It's so good to see you again. And to meet your daughter, especially when she is the bearer of such good news."

Rachel beamed.

Pamela looked around the table. "Some of you already know this, but for anyone who doesn't, Rachel and her friend identified the woman who impersonated me and stole my identity. Unfortunately, the woman was killed two days ago in Florida, but—well, Rachel, tell everyone what happened?"

Unused to being the center of attention, Rachel felt her cheeks get hot. She cleared her throat and relayed what she and Zach had done, including the FRS mugshot of Jocelyn Warner that popped up. "We also know she was working with a partner, but we haven't been able to identify him yet." She heard the sound of a door opening. "However, we think it's just a matter of time. The desk clerk at the resort where they stayed gave the police a detailed description."

"The young lady is absolutely correct," a new voice piped up.

Rachel turned toward the door. Two men had just entered the conference room. The first was a young, apple-cheeked man in glasses who fit the stereotype of a geek with a pocket protector so well she could see the bulge under his jacket. The other, older but taller, was strangely familiar. He was casually dressed, in khakis, a buttoned down shirt, and a windbreaker. Rachel glanced over at her mother, who was staring open-mouthed at the man.

The man grinned. "Hello, Ellie. You don't look a minute older, *cher*." This time it was her mother whose face turned crimson. The man, his hand outstretched, went to Pamela Cannon. "I'm Nick LeJeune, FBI Special Agent. And this is Special Agent Carl Forrester from the Cyber Security Division." He gestured to Pocket Protector.

"Well, I see you already know some of us. Pleased to meet you, Mr. LeJeune. And Forrester. Please, sit down."

Forrester promptly sat down, but Agent LeJeune strolled around to the tray of breakfast pastries and took his time selecting a donut and pouring coffee. When he came to the table, he glanced over at Rachel and winked.

It was the wink that did it. *Holy shit,* Rachel thought. *I remember now.* Agent LeJeune had helped her mother a long time ago when she was mixed up with the Mafia and a guy who'd been in one of her videos but was later murdered. Her mother told her LeJeune was part Cajun, as tasty as barbecue and just as spicy. They'd had some kind of personal relationship too, but what Rachel remembered was his car, a Porche Spyder. He'd taken her for a ride—she must have been about thirteen—and for that she'd considered him coolness personified.

Now, as an adult, she studied him. He was tall, lean, with short gray hair and deep green eyes. Crow's feet creased the skin around his eyes when he smiled, and the stubble on his chin, still in vogue, told Rachel he still wanted to look good. He didn't have to worry about that. He did.

"Hi Nick," Rachel said. "How's the Spyder?" Then she made eye contact with her mother. She hadn't said a word since he came in and still appeared to be flustered.

"Good memory, Rachel." He chuckled and scratched his nose. "But I traded it in ten years ago. For a Benz." His accent was still definitely Southern. S's that sounded like z's, as if he were talking around a marble in his mouth. But he'd lived in Chicago at least fifteen years. Was he exaggerating the lilt?

He turned back to Pamela. "Ma'am, I don't want to take up any more of your time with chit-chat. Let me just say that you have a very sharp set of eyes working for you. She nailed the woman. In fact Miss Foreman and her friend discovered her identity before we did. And she's correct about Warner having a partner." He smiled. "Special Agent Forrester and his team have all night. They were able to identify him. He's Steven Morgan, originally from Terra Haute, Indiana." He nodded at Forrester, who got up and passed two photos around the table.

"He likely hacked into your bank accounts," LeJeune said. "He's pretty handy with a mouse and a monitor. Makes his living on identity theft. We have a national BOLO on him, and even though he used an alias, we think we've tracked his rental car via GPS. We should have an update later today." He smiled. "And, of course, you have been totally exonerated from anything having to do with the murder of Fields."

Pamela Cannon smiled. "Why that's wonderful. Great work, everyone!" She started clapping, and everyone in the room joined in. "So, who is going to untangle the mess with my bank accounts, password, and Social Security number?"

"Ma'am," LeJeune said, "Since the case is now in our laps, so to speak, we'll take it from here."

"Good. How long will it take to restore my identity?"

"Hard to say. We need to assess how much damage was done. But I'd say in a month's time, you'll see a lot of improvement."

Pamela nodded. "Excellent. So that leaves just one other question. Well, two." She paused and looked around the room. "Who the hell killed the Warner woman? And why?"

Chapter 20

B raids of sparkling Italian lights on the ceiling cast a warm, celebratory glow over Amalfi, a new Italian restaurant in Evanston. Rachel, Zach, and Ellie relaxed over glasses of red wine and appetizers of calamari, shrimp, and mussels.

"So, how does it feel to be exonerated?" Ellie asked.

"I can't believe it," Rachel said. "It really happened."

"Yes, it did." Her mother smiled. "I saw her pull you aside just before we left. What did she say?"

Rachel paused and sipped her wine. "I'm not sure I should tell you."

"Why not?"

"She said it was private."

"Oh." Ellie's brow furrowed. "In that case..." She shrugged. "Far be it from me to pry a secret out of my daughter."

Rachel laughed. "Mom, you've done that your whole life." She looked over at Zach.

"I'm not touching that with a ten foot pole."

"Smart guy," Ellie shot back.

"Okay, okay," Rachel said. "I'll tell you. She said she was

impressed with my initiative and problem-solving skills and told me if I ever wanted to work at Carefill there would be a home for me."

"Really?" Ellie brightened. "How wonderful!"

"You're telling me," Rachel said.

"Well?"

"Well, what?"

"Well, are you going to take her up on it?"

"Carefill?"

"No. Standard Oil. Of course, Carefill."

"I don't know." Rachel looked over at Zach. "I like what I'm doing."

"Yes, but—" Ellie broke off.

"Yes, but I'm not making any money. That's what you were going to say, right Mom?"

Ellie shrugged.

"By the way, Mom, is there anything you want to tell me?"

"About what?"

"How about Special Agent Nick LeJeune?"

"Now, wait a minute, Rachel. I—"

The waiter appeared, ending the conversation. "Have you decided what you'd like this evening? Or shall I tell you about the specials?"

When dinner was over, Zach and Rachel walked Joshua, who'd been visiting Rachel's apartment. Afterwards they climbed up to the third floor of her Greystone. Zach drew her into his arms and kissed her. Rachel let herself get lost in the moment. With Zach it was easy. They broke apart and Rachel fumbled for her key, so distracted that she had to stab the lock several times before it slipped into the keyhole.

Zach came in and sat on the couch. Joshua flopped down beside him and panted. The dog gave off a damp, furry smell, but Rachel didn't mind.

"Did you mean what you said at dinner?" Zach asked.

"About what?"

"About being happy doing what you're doing."

"Can't you tell?"

He shrugged. "I'm not sure. It's only been about three weeks since we met."

She wriggled into the tiny space on the couch next to Zach and the dog. "I know. That's what frigging amazes me." Zach cocked his head. "Three weeks, and I feel like I've known you—No, that's trite. What I mean is—well, it's just so much fun— no..." Rachel's voice trailed off. She felt herself blush from the neck up.

Zach leaned over and kissed her, one of those kisses that tingled and took her breath away. When they parted, he said, "I know what you mean. I feel the same way."

"Really?"

"I look forward to you coming over every morning. And I want to see you every night. And I can't wait until the next morning when you get there."

Rachel was quiet for a moment. Then she blew out a breath. "No one's ever said that to me before."

"No one's ever made me want to say it."

The hint of a smile came over Rachel. "So what do we do?"

"You let Joshua and me stay with you tonight so we don't have to wait."

"Hmm." Her smile widened. She stood up, took Zach's hand, and led him into her bedroom. Joshua stayed on the couch.

Chapter 21

Three weeks later

Pamela Cannon felt rested and hopeful as she entered the Carefill building in Chicago's Loop early on a bright Friday morning in May. Three weeks had passed since the "incident," as she called it, and the efforts to steal her identity had failed. Thanks to the FBI, her new passport was now secure, as well as her Social Security number. Her bank accounts had been restored, and the man behind the hacking, Steven Morgan, had been caught.

He'd been hiding out in the Florida Panhandle. When Florida State Police cornered him, Morgan, facing a life sentence for the murder of Donald Fields, pulled out a 38 Special, aimed, and fired. The police fired back, and he was pronounced dead at a Tallahassee hospital. According to the FBI, Morgan had once been an up and coming IT staffer at a Fortune 500 company, but the lure of easy money had turned him into what Special Agent LeJeune called a two-bit hacker.

"Why did he kill Donald Fields, Agent LeJeune?" Pamela asked. "And how did they know each other?"

"As far as we can tell, Fields wanted revenge on you for firing him, so he found—"

"He was stealing money from Carefill, I forced him to pay restitution, and *he* wanted revenge?" she said. "He was lucky I didn't turn him over to the police."

"Ma'am, some people see themselves as victims no matter what life offers up." LeJeune shrugged. "Honestly, at this point we're not sure how Fields and Morgan hooked up, but we've got Morgan's laptop. We'll find out." He paused. "As for why Morgan and the woman killed him, we think they wanted to cut him out of the deal. They wanted your money for themselves."

Pamela had to be satisfied with that explanation for the time being. She still didn't know why the Warner woman was killed, but that wasn't her problem. In fact, she smiled as she tapped the elevator button. She would be flying to Vienna for a meeting tomorrow, and then she'd fly to Brussels to visit Laurie.

Her good mood evaporated once she walked into Carefill's corporate headquarters. The receptionist was talking to someone, and her frantic expression said something was very wrong. Outside her own office Kelly huddled behind her desk with Devin, Stan, and a couple of IT engineers. Everyone was pointing fingers at Kelly's monitor and trying to talk at the same time. When they saw Pamela, as if on cue, everyone froze.

Devin cleared his throat. "The FBI are on their way over."

"Why?" Pamela's heart rate quickened so fast she thought she could hear it in her ears. "What's happened?"

The group exchanged glances, then Devin led her into her office to her computer. "Look."

Her monitor was completely red. One of those warning signs you see on highways, a white triangle with an exclamation point inside was prominent. Underneath were the words "Your files are encrypted.

All your company documents and other important files have been locked with a unique key. You cannot retrieve anything until you comply with our demands. A white box with red letters said "Click here."

Pamela hugged her arms. "What happens when you click?"

Devin gestured. "Go ahead. It responds to the password of the person using the computer."

A sinking wave of horror came over Pamela. She did not want to tap anything. She glared at Kevin, moused across the screen, and tapped a key. A still photo of her daughter Laurie filled the monitor. She was seated on a chair. Wearing a business suit. A gag was tied around her mouth. In her hands was a copy of the International New York Times with today's date on it. The background of the photo was white. Nothing but white.

Pamela felt her throat close up. She tried to suck in a breath but couldn't. "What is this?" she was finally able to ask. On one level she knew, but she refused to accept it. Laurie held a senior position at the World Bank, where her mission was to develop the economies of third world countries. Pamela was incredibly proud of her daughter, but rarely talked about her. Laurie preferred to keep a low profile, and Pamela respected her for it.

"Kelly, did you call her at the Bank? They're seven hours ahead of us."

"Yes ma'am. She hasn't been in all day."

Pamela felt her composure slip. A peculiar lightheaded, airy sensation filled her. At the same time, she knew she had to get a grasp of the situation. Compartmentalize. Become the rational CEO she was known to be. She couldn't afford to panic like normal mothers who would have begged the authorities to do or say anything and everything to get their daughters home safely. This attack was not only an attack on her, but also on the company. Pamela raised her hand to her forehead and turned away from the group. "Give me a moment."

Stan's voice was compassionate but firm. "Pam, you don't have a minute. Hit the space bar."

A message popped up. "Be at your desk by nine AM sharp. We will contact you."

Pamela looked at the clock hanging on the opposite wall. It was eight-fifteen.

Chapter 22

8:30 AM

Special agents Nick LeJeune and Carl Forrester arrived by eight-thirty. They'd been briefed by Devin on the way over.

LeJeune got right down to business. "Ma'am, Agent Forrester needs to look at your computer."

"Fine, as long as he finishes by nine."

"Yes ma'am. We know."

Forrester sat down and tapped through the three sequenced messages. He looked over at Kelly. "Did you get all three of these as well?"

"No," Kelly answered. "Just one and two."

"So they've been able to manipulate who sees what," Forrester said almost to himself. "Pretty sophisticated."

"Have you contacted any other departments on your network?" LeJeune asked.

Devin answered. "First thing I did. Everyone's affected."

"Internationally?"

Devin nodded. "No one who works for Carefill can do anything. IT's been fielding calls since last night."

"Why didn't you call me then?" Pamela asked.

"We thought it was just a DDOS. It happens. We have pretty damn good firewalls, though, and can usually deal with them. This time was different."

"How?"

"This was a full scale attack. Someone got in and took control of the root system. Probably through an unsecured port they found to wiggle into."

"Wait," Pamela said. "You're way ahead of me."

Devin explained about incoming and outgoing ports. They were analogous to back doors. How a company like Carefill had hundreds of thousands of them. Most were secure; he'd made sure of that. But there could always be a few that were missed. With access through one port hackers could penetrate the system. In time, if they were good, they could cripple it.

LeJeune turned to Forrester. "Any initial thoughts Carl?"

"Not yet. Maybe during the call... " His voice trailed off.

LeJeune said, "We'll be listening in, recording, and tracing it. Got that going before we left the Bureau."

"What will that do? If they're smart enough to attack an entire company without us knowing who they are?" Pamela said.

"It's protocol whenever there's a ransomware attack. Who's your head of IT?"

"That would be me," Devin said.

"We want to figure out how and where these creeps got in. Will you help them get situated?"

"Get who situated?" Devin asked.

"Our team of Bureau hackers."

"Of course," he waved helplessly. "Can they override the ransomware?"

Forrester spoke up. "Probably not. At least, not right now. But they'll study every incoming and outgoing port."

"Excuse me, gentlemen, but I'd like to add a couple of people to the team," she said.

"Who's that, ma'am?" LeJeune asked.

"The young man who works with Rachel and Ellie Foreman. They identified the woman who was killed before you or Chicago police. That won't be a problem will it? I believe you have some history with them, correct?"

LeJeune seemed to be taken aback for a moment. Then he shot her a sly grin. "Of course, Ms. Cannon. We'd be pleased to add them. I'll take care of it."

Everyone looked at the clock. Ten minutes before nine.

"Agent LeJeune, could this be connected to the murder of that woman in Florida?" Pamela asked.

"I don't know, ma'am." His Southern lilt was beginning to irritate her. She pushed it aside. "But if it is, we'll find out."

Chapter 23

8:50 AM

Pamela watched the clock's hands crawl forward. Time stretched out, and the ten minutes before the call felt like ten days. She sat quietly, her fingers tightly laced together on her desk, while a whirlwind of activity blew around her. Her executives barked into their cells, Forrester made some kind of notations on his, and Kelly stood stock still as if panic had turned her into a pillar of salt.

The only person who seemed at ease was LeJeune, who was also on his cell, presumably calling Rachel Foreman. Pamela supposed that was a positive. She recalled the quotation, "If you can keep your head when all about you are losing theirs and blaming it on you." Kipling wrote it, she thought. Then she reproached herself for thinking something so cerebral when her daughter's life was in danger.

She couldn't lose Laurie. Her husband Phillip's death from cancer had sliced her heart open, and she never completely recovered. She knew she would never remarry. But to lose her daughter, too? God couldn't be that cruel. He or She, as she preferred to think, should take Pamela instead. Laurie, whose life and career were blossoming, should have years—no, decades— of rich, fulfilling experiences.

She glanced at the clock. Three minutes left. The clock's second hand seemed to slow even more. People in the room stopped talking. All of them stared at the clock. Pamela shivered. What if the attackers had timed an explosion for 9 AM? What if everyone in her office room was counting down their doom? She forced herself to reject the idea. Of course that couldn't happen. Whoever was behind this wanted something, something they wouldn't get it if they killed her. She squeezed her eyes shut.

She wasn't sure how much time had passed when her phone chirped. She flung open her eyes. and watched the flashing yellow button. Then she cleared her throat and answered, activating the speakerphone as she did.

"This is Pamela Cannon," she said evenly, as if this was just another call.

9:00 AM

"Good morning Ms. Cannon," The voice was tinny and robotic. It had been disguised. Pamela was unable to determine whether it was female or male.

"To whom am I speaking?" she asked.

The voice replied, "That's not important." A pause. "What is important is that you do what we say."

"And what is it you want?" Pamela looked at Devin and Stan when she asked the question.

"The Project."

"What project?" Pamela said.

"Don't be coy."

The color drained from her face. "How did you—"

"As I said, don't be coy. If you want to see your daughter again, you will send us the formula."

"I'm not in a position to—"

"We will not waste time debating. You have twenty-four hours to decide." The voice disconnected.

9:10 AM

The pressure in the room deflated, as if a giant balloon had been untied. With it went some of the tension. The atmosphere wasn't thick with relief, but it was a lowering of temperature.

Pamela glanced around. "Let's adjourn to the conference room."

As she rose from her desk, her phone chirped again. She froze, along with everyone else, then cautiously pressed the speaker button. The receptionist announced that the Foremans and Mr. Dolan had arrived. Pamela let out a breath and told the receptionist to take them to the conference room.

A few minutes later when everyone was assembled, Pamela said, "I'm going to explain a few things. Then I'd like everyone's opinion about what we should do."

She folded her hands. "About seven years ago, just after I became CEO, we invested heavily to find a cure for Alzheimer's disease. Carefill's founder, James Kilbourne died from it. So did my father. It's one of the reasons I chose to work for a pharmaceutical company. There is nothing more important to me than working towards a cure or a vaccine for that horrible, dehumanizing disease."

She gazed around the room. "We started with a task force, assembling all the research we could find from everywhere in the world. As you can imagine, that in itself took over two years. Not to mention everything that has been published or touted in the press since. Some of the research was solid; some was from kooks. It didn't matter. The task force looked at everything. To put it in perspective, over 200 failed trials of different substances have been attempted to cure this insidious disease. Billions of dollars spent. Nothing has worked. Stan Trollop was—is—part of that task force."

Stan dipped his head in acknowledgement.

"With the advent of gene therapy, a new approach opened up, and we began to make headway. Of course, everything was top secret. We didn't want our competitors to know what we were doing, and we didn't want to announce anything before we were ready. We called it 'The Project,' and we were very careful with who knew what.

"About two years ago, R&D came up with a promising lead at the cellular level. Researchers have long debated whether Alzheimer's is caused by a virus or other infection that settles in brain cells and then produces the beta-amyloid chemical. Beta-amyloid interferes with the virus, but when combined with it, it destroys the brain cells themselves. To make a long story short, about a year ago, we came up with an anti-viral that, at least in mice, works."

She paused and looked around again. "We were very close to starting clinical trials." She smiled ruefully. "At that point, however, we knew we would lose our anonymity. The FDA and other authorities had to be notified, and although they're supposed to keep the studies confidential, well..." She grimaced. "...you know how well the government keeps secrets.

"So, we decided to, in a way, go rogue. To stay under the radar as long as possible until we knew if the trials were safe and effective. We knew we could submit them to the FDA as a fait accompli. We found a remote area near Lucerne, Switzerland and set up the lab and clinic. And now, despite all our efforts, it's clear some... motherfuckers... with sophisticated technology already know what we're doing and want it for themselves."

Until now Pamela had managed to keep her emotions at bay, but now her eyes filled and her voice cracked. "And now I'm being forced to make the most excruciating decision any mother could ever contemplate."

Chapter 24

Pamela leaned back and covered her eyes with her hand. Watching Pamela's misery, Rachel felt a lump thicken her throat. Zach squeezed her hand under the table. She gave a grateful squeeze back.

Agent LeJeune had been making notes on a legal pad while Cannon spoke. Now he cleared his throat and stood up. "Okay, friends. We have a series of complex tasks to perform." His tone was studiously gentle. "And the lack of time makes it critical that everyone does their job. We'll divide up in teams to attack different angles of the situation. We have the cyber forensics guys standing by at the Bureau, and they'll be quite helpful, but because of the time, we're gonna need all the arms and legs we can muster."

"What's your plan?" Cannon asked.

"As I said, we have several angles to investigate. Number one: the relationship between the caller this morning and Steven Morgan. Are they on the same side? If they are, how are they related?"

Devin spoke up. "They have to be; each one executed a distinct stage of the attack."

"If they were allies, then why was the Warner woman killed? Did Warner and Morgan even know about the Project? Or were they only interested only in Cannon's money? We never heard a peep about your Project from them.

"Number two. There was a relationship between Donald Fields and Morgan. How did they find each other? Who initiated contact? And how? Through his email? A phishing scam?"

"I can work on that," Zach said. "It stands to reason whoever locked down the Carefill system might have found a back door through Fields' email."

"Great," LeJeune said. "Carl, you have Fields' home computer. Get a clone to Zach ASAP."

"Can do."

Zach grinned.

LeJeune grinned back. "See what you can find, Buddy. You have Kali Linux?"

"Of course."

"See if you can figure out how Fields hooked up with Morgan. Or was it the other way around? Was the woman a honey trap? We have Morgan's laptop too, and Cyber will look for any connections between Morgan, Fields, and the assholes who are attacking Carefill."

Zach nodded.

LeJeune turned to Rachel. "We need to go through the research Carefill collected when they started the Project. It's entirely possible you'll find some source or some individual who was asking questions that were slightly off."

"What do you mean?" Rachel asked.

"It's hard to describe. Something that doesn't fit. Something that makes you say, huh? Why is this issue being raised? Ellie, you know what I'm talking about, right? It might get us, directly or indirectly, closer to whoever is fucking with Carefill."

"I'll work with her," Ellie said. "Once she's on her way, I'll come back here in case something else comes up. What about you, Nick?"

"I'll contact Interpol and the Swiss authorities to see if they can help find Laurie, *cher.*"Ellie got a *cher*, Rachel noted. Her mother's face flushed.

"But don't come back here. We'll meet virtually instead. Saves time."

Pamela Cannon stood. She seemed to have regained her composure. "Thank you, everyone. Let me know what you need. Anything at all."

"We'll meet in three hours." LeJeune looked at his watch. "One PM. Virtually. We'll use the FBI's video conference platform. It's secure. We'll call you with the link. Oh, and don't text or email us. They're probably watching us, or gearing up to."

He went on. "Ms. Cannon, call your Swiss clinic. Make sure it hasn't been compromised in any way. Are their systems connected to yours here at Carefill?"

Devin spoke up. "No. Completely separate."

"That's good news. Still, you should check. Which reminds me. Zach, if you get any traces or even suspicion that someone is onto you, let me know ASAP. Two can play that game."

"Sure thing."

Before they left, Rachel saw Zach in deep conversation with Carl Forrester. When it ended, they nodded at each other.

Chapter 25

"What's Kali Linux?" Rachel asked when they were back at his office with the clone of Fields' hard drive.

"It's software for the good guys. It has lots of tools we can use to get into systems, crack passwords, detect firewalls that aren't up to snuff, things like that."

"Can I learn it?" Rachel asked.

"Maybe. But there are things you have to learn first. Like basic programming."

"Barkus is willing," she said.

"Huh?" He frowned and shot her a sideways glance, as if she'd spoken another language, but when she sneaked a peek at her mother, Ellie was grinning. Zach looked at Ellie too, then back at Rachel. "Wait. This is some weird mother-daughter thing, right?"

Both Ellie and Rachel laughed. Then Ellie said, "Let's get to work. Which machines should we use?"

Zach got them on two of his Macs before he sat behind his console and started tapping keys. Ellie and Rachel copied a flash drive given to them by Stan Trollop before they left. On it were five folders. "Let's divide them up," Ellie said. "There's probably a ton of material in each."

"What am I looking for?"

"It's hard to say, but we can make some commonsense assumptions. Anything from a university or well-known medical journal probably *isn't* what we're looking for. Those studies or opinions or whatever they are would have been pored over by Carefill scientists."

"Because of their credibility."

"Exactly." Ellie tapped on one of the folders. "We're not looking for kooky stuff, you know, someone who says they can cure Alzheimer's with crystals or chicken soup." She paused. "But anything that was written or published by a legitimate researcher might lead somewhere. Some small random study, for example. Or a doctor or scientist with lots of initials after his name."

"Why? I don't get it."

"Maybe the paper was ignored by the 'establishment' Alzheimer's community, and the author is angry about being overlooked. Or maybe the study was too small to be included in the bigger pools of research, and the people who produced it want recognition. We don't have a lot of time, but we should try to be as thorough as we can. Does that help?"

"Sort of." Rachel ran a tongue around her lips.

"Tell you what. Let's go through the first folder together. You'll see what I'm talking about."

Rachel nodded, and Ellie pulled a chair up to her computer. Rachel opened one of the five folders, which was labelled "Alzheimer's Association." Inside was another folder with the label "Grants 2008-2020." Rachel hovered and clicked on "2008." Over 130 projects were partially or totally funded by the Association, out of over 600 application proposals.

"That's a lot of grants. Do we need to look at all of them?" Rachel asked.

"I don't think so. If they've been funded, it means they were credible. It might be nice if we could scan the application proposals, though. Could give us a lead."

Rachel moused around the folder. "They're not here. Just the subject criteria from which they made their decisions."

Ellie replied. "Let's see. That might help."

Rachel read out loud. "Beta-amyloid, Tau, and related proteins... the toxic properties of beta-amyloid... What's beta amyloid?"

"That's a sticky protein that grows in the brain and interferes with communication between cells. Many people think it's a huge indicator, maybe even the cause, of Alzheimer's."

"Thanks." Rachel went back to the list of subjects. "The effect of the disease on brain neurons... inflammation, blood vessels... tools for earlier and more accurate diagnosis..." Her eyes widened. "Jeez. Get your science degree in four hours."

"Better get started."

The three of them worked in silence for the next two hours. After a while, Rachel observed subtle patterns and changes in how grants and studies were funded. By 2019 more epidemiological studies were given grants. The same was true in a new subject area of "novel treatment strategies."

That gave Rachel an idea, and she Googled "novel Alzheimer's treatments." A new drug was showing promise and was in the human trials stage. Other researchers were looking at gum disease as a possible cause. Others thought the spice turmeric could help destroy beta-amyloid in the brain. Even a Chinese drug that changes the microbiome in the gut to reduce brain inflammation was in trials. Rachel wrote down the scientists and doctors involved. She would call them.

She was on the tenth page of Google results when she scanned a report from a geneticist from Atlanta, Georgia. Written thirty years earlier, it concerned Vietnam Vets who developed early onset Alzheimer's. She was reading it more carefully, when Zach suddenly yelled. "Oh no you don't, asshole!"

Chapter 26

R achel whipped around. "What's happening, Zach?"
"Hold on a sec," he tapped rapidly on his keyboard, then shut the machine down. "Do me a favor. Shut down your computers. Now."

"Is everything okay?" Ellie asked.

"I think so," Zach replied. "They're good, these attackers. They have NSA grade stuff." He sucked in a breath. "Crap."

"What's going on?"

"Shut everything down. Now!" He was almost shouting.

"Done!" Ellie said.

"Me too. Calm down," Rachel said.

Once their computers were off, he said, "So here's what happened. The first thing I did was load Fields' hard drive onto my computer and open his email program."

"How did you get the password?" Rachel asked.

"Used the password cracker on Kali Linux. It only took a few minutes."

"Wow." She raised her eyebrows.

"His email included emails from Josie Warner, the woman with Morgan who was shot on the beach."

"Right."

"I texted LeJeune with her info, although I'm sure his forensics team already has it. Then I looked around for his Carefill email account. Most employees who work for corporations have their work email on their personal devices too, right?"

"Right again," Ellie said.

"Sure enough, there it was. In Account Preferences. I was able to crack that password too." Zach leaned back and stretched out his arms. "That's when it got interesting."

"What was there?"

"What and who," Zach replied. "So I scanned back a couple of months to when Fields was still at Carefill, embezzling money. In January, I came across an email that said, 'We know what you're doing.'"

"That was all?" Rachel said.

"That was it. No ID as to who it was, and the return email didn't exist. I can't show you because of what just happened."

"Which was..." Ellie said.

"I think I found the back door that allowed the attackers into Carefill's system."

"How?"

"It looked like a phishing email. Fields should have known better, but because he actually was doing something illegal, he must have been scared as hell that someone knew what he was up to. So, of course, he clicked on the email." Zach looked from Rachel to Ellie. "That's how they got in."

"It's that simple?" Ellie said.

"Yes and no. It doesn't mean they got control right away. The hackers probably had to work for months. They had to grab admin privileges at each stage of their penetration. But they were patient and they worked carefully. Eventually they got control over the entire Carefill system."

"And no one knew they were there?" Rachel asked.

"Nope. They disguised themselves, electronically speaking, moving laterally across the system, until they got what they wanted."

Rachel swallowed. "That's unbelievable."

Zach continued. "Fields was fired in March, right?"

Rachel nodded.

"So theoretically, his email account went dormant. The black hat hackers probably used the dormant account as their portal. But that's not the most important thing."

"What is?"

"They knew I was in there just now. Someone was watching me try to track *them*."

Horror washed across Rachel's face. "How do you know?"

"Everything on my machine slowed down. My cursor started to move on its own. And when I checked my CPU, it was at 100 percent usage. That's crazy. I only had a couple of apps open. They were hacking *me*."

"How did they know you were there?"

"When they began their penetration, they probably installed a keyboard logger to monitor every keystroke. It would let them know if someone who shouldn't be there somehow hacked in. That's what I would have done."

"No!" Ellie cried.

Zach nodded. "I got out of there pronto, but they either already got my IP address or they'll have it soon. Which means they'll figure out who I am. And, by extension, you too, babe."

A look of alarm came over Ellie. She glanced at Rachel. "Not again."

Chapter 27

1:00 PM

The group met promptly at one that afternoon on the FBI's virtual video conferencing platform. It was a lot like Zoom but more secure. Ellie and Rachel shared one screen, Zach another. LeJeune, Forrester, Pamela, her two executives, and Kelly were each on his or her own screen.

LeJeune spoke first. "So let's bring each other up to speed. I'll go first. We talked to Interpol, and a three-man team is driving to Lucerne to make sure the testing site is secure. They'll let us know what they find. Another team in Brussels is combing through your daughter's workplace and apartment, searching for anything that could tell us where she is."

Pamela blinked. "Thank you."

"I'll be up front with you, Ms. Cannon. Don't get your hopes up. If these people are as careful IRL as they are online—"

"IRL?" Pamela cut in.

"In real life, ma'am. I don't anticipate we'll find much. They're meticulous. At least their hackers are."

"I understand," Pamela said.

LeJeune continued. "Zach, you said you had something."

Zach explained how he'd tried to back into the Carefill network using the phishing email sent to Fields. "I figured it was a fifty-fifty shot, but I didn't make it. They spotted me. Had to shut down."

"Damn," LeJeune said. "I knew they were good. But the ability to track you after, what—how long were you in there?"

"Less than five minutes. They must have a keyboard logger."

"Damage assessment?"

"It's a good bet they know who I am."

LeJeune frowned. "Which means they might also find Rachel. Or Ellie."

Zach nodded.

"I don't like it, *cher*," LeJeune said to Ellie. "I think you two might need a safe house."

"Oh, come on, Nick," Ellie countered. "We're not spies."

"But *they* could be." He paused. "And with Rachel's history..."

Rachel ran a hand through her hair. "I'll be fine. Really. I did learn a thing or two at the police academy."

"You're telling me you're armed?" LeJeune asked.

"If I need to be." She shot her mother a warning glance. She hoped her mother wouldn't overreact. Guns didn't scare Rachel like they did her mother. In fact, Rachel was a different person in the five years since *she'd* been kidnapped. She was stronger. More confident and able to take care of herself. The Academy had taught her that, even though she had dropped out.

"Okay. We'll talk more later," LeJeune said. "Carl, what about any connections between the caller this morning, Fields, and Morgan?"

Carl, whose presence on the call was just a name in white on a tiny black screen, suddenly appeared in person. He must have been working on his laptop while LeJeune was talking, Rachel thought. "We found a link between Fields and Morgan."

"Yeah? How?"

"Fields found Morgan on the dark web. One of those shopping sites that offer illegal black market services."

"Really."

"They went into a private chat room to discuss the job. Morgan gave him a hard time. Dangled him on a string for about a week. Fields was practically foaming at the mouth by then. Finally, Morgan said okay."

"You have the correspondence?"

"Yep. As a matter of fact, Morgan pretended to be a woman. Said her name was Josie."

"Bingo." LeJeune smiled for the first time that day.

"Morgan was in IT, remember? The woman was just a two-bit grifter."

"And a little lagniappe for Morgan," LeJeune snorted.

"Nick," Ellie retorted. "That's pretty sexist for an FBI agent."

He glared at Ellie but kept his mouth shut.

Pamela Cannon spoke up. "Great work, Carl."

"It was a team effort with our Cyber Security Division, ma'am."

"Please give them my gratitude." She paused. "But what about the connection to the caller this morning? And the ransomware? That's our priority, isn't it?"

"Of course, ma'am. We're looking into that."

"So, nothing yet."

"We're just starting, Ms. Cannon." LeJeune took over. He looked at Zach, who twisted around and stared at Rachel.

She knew that was her cue. "Mom and I went through most of the research. There are a couple of people I want to follow up with."

"And?"

"I'll call them right after this meeting."

"I might be able to play around inside the network a little more," Zach offered. "Who knows? Maybe they forgot to mask themselves somewhere along the way and we can identify their IP address."

"And let me see what Interpol found," LeJeune said. "They'll work through the night."

Pamela's expression went dark. Rachel could tell she knew they were nowhere near cracking the case. Yet.

Chapter 28

"So you have a gun at home?" Ellie asked after the call.

"You think I got a permit for nothing?" Rachel replied. "Of course I do."

"'Of course?' What do you mean, of course? What kind of gun?"

"Mom, that really isn't any of your business, you know?"

"I raised you to be afraid of guns. I never thought you'd ever have one in your apartment. It's way too easy to use it during times of—well—stress. Or conflict."

"Maybe for you," Rachel said. "No. Wait, I'm sorry. That wasn't fair." She tucked a lock of hair behind her ear and tried again. "You taught me well. And I appreciate it. In fact, the Academy taught me pretty much the same thing. Believe me, I have tremendous respect for my weapon. It is not something to be trifled with. I would never use it except in a life or death situation. Which I hope never, ever happens." She went to her mother and gave her a hug. "Look. Neither of us expected that I would be kidnapped. Or go through the things that happened as a result. That *was* life and death. It won't ever happen again."

Ellie returned the hug and smiled. "How did you turn out to be so wise and thoughtful and brave?"

"I had you for a mother?"

Her mother laughed. "And such an apple-polisher."

After Zach ordered out for sandwiches, Ellie decided to drive back downtown to Carefill's headquarters. Zach took Joshua out for a walk while Rachel started her calls. The first was to Ken Drier, whose byline was on the article about gum disease. Rachel had prepared an explanation that was accurate, as far as it went.

"Hello. I'm doing some research for a client about Alzheimer's disease, and your name came up as someone who wrote an article about its links to gum disease."

Drier wasn't a scientist or a researcher. He was a freelance writer who picked up the article via an online writers' consortium. Apparently a study of brain tissue from Alzheimer patients who died found a link between specific bacteria that cause gum disease and Alzheimer's. "Turns out it's nothing to get excited about," he said. "Just as many scientists who say there's a link say there isn't."

"What's the name of the bacteria?" Rachel asked.

"*P. gingivalis*," Drier said. "But the links haven't been replicated in other studies, and one study isn't enough to establish cause and effect."

"Were the scientists mentioned in your article about Alzheimer's specialists?"

He laughed. "I talked to more dentists than Alzheimer's researchers for that article. But, you know, all in a day's work."

"Okay, thanks." Rachel hung up. It wasn't a promising lead, but she wrote down the researchers' name in the article.

She looked out the window. Zach and Joshua were jogging around a tiny pond across the street from his office building. The sun glinted off the water, triggering sunbeams that made Rachel long to join them. Maybe they could all take a walk later.

No. Who was she kidding? The stakes were too high and the time too short. They would be working 24-7 until the kidnapping was resolved, one way or the other.

She recalled her own kidnapping five years ago. After she'd survived and come home, she was so emotionally overwrought that she'd never asked her mother exactly whom she'd reached out to and what they'd done to find her. Were her mother's efforts as organized, methodical, and nerve-wracking as what they were doing now? Maybe she'd ask her mother sometime, although she had a feeling Ellie wouldn't want to relive any of it. If it had been her own child, Rachel wouldn't want to either.

She went back to her notes. Her second call was to the M.D. who reviewed an article on a website that claimed turmeric could influence brain changes in Alzheimer patients. Apparently the curcumin in the spice curbed inflammation and combatted oxidative stress, two factors that could contribute to Alzheimer's disease. Like the first article, however, the studies were not replicated. In fact, further studies refuted it.

She got up, stretched, and did some jumping jacks. Then she sat back down. Zach and Joshua came back in. Joshua bounded up to her, tail wagging, waiting for her to praise him. She leaned down and ruffled his fur. "What a good boy you are."

Joshua nuzzled his head in her lap.

"My turn?" Zach joked.

She shot him a glance. "You know what I love about dogs?"

"What?"

"They don't talk back. Or tell bad jokes."

She went back to her cell. Her third call was to a doctor in Atlanta, Richard Hookie. He'd had an interest in Alzheimer's a long time ago, and the report she read said he was studying a link to Agent Orange, a poisonous defoliant used by the US during the Vietnam War which sickened soldiers. Rachel got his assistant and left her name.

"Who was that?" Zach asked.

"Hookie, the Vietnam Vet. He was out to lunch. His assistant said he'd call back."

Chapter 29

2:00 PM

D r. Richard Hookie, or Hook, finished his corned beef hash and salad. He grabbed a toothpick on the way out of the restaurant. He wasn't much of a cook, at least not nowadays, so he ate his main meal for lunch. Dinner was lighter: scrambled eggs, a sandwich, or even popcorn occasionally, although he was careful about salt. He walked back to the lab. May was the unofficial start of a long wet-hot summer in Georgia, but a cloud cover today made it bearable.

Back in the lab his assistant, Donna, handed him his messages. Only three today, one from a medical student, another from a colleague, and a third from someone named Rachel Foreman in Chicago. She was working on a time-sensitive matter; could he return her call ASAP? Intrigued, he went to his office instead of the lab and called her back.

Zach answered. "Dolan here."

"This is Dr. Richard Hookie. I'm looking for Rachel Foreman."

"One moment." The call went to hold. Three seconds later, a

woman's voice answered. "Dr. Hookie, thank you so much for calling back."

"You said it was time-sensitive. What can I do for you?"

Rachel recited her prepared explanation. "I'm doing some research for a client about Alzheimer's disease, and your name came up as someone who at one time was studying it yourself."

"Really? Who told you that?"

Rachel had the article ready. "It's a report from about thirty years ago. About Vietnam Vets who had developed early-onset Alzheimer's. From Tulane."

"Well, I'll be. I completely forgot about that report. You did your homework."

"Thank you sir. I just have a couple of questions."

"Sure. Go ahead."

"At the time you thought Alzheimer's was a virus. Do you still believe that?"

"Of course. Most scientists do. Or, let me put it this way. Somehow, a virus is activated. We still don't know how."

"You thought maybe Agent Orange had something to do with it, correct?"

"I did. But I couldn't prove it. Most people in the field thought it was a stretch. But, you never know. Agent Orange had so many poisonous chemicals in it, I'm still concerned that it might have burrowed into human beings in a mutated form."

"Why didn't you pursue it?"

"Two reasons. One, everyone and their mother was researching Alzheimer's. And many of them were much farther along than I was. At the time, my theory was way out there. So I decided to focus on something that could make a tangible difference. Like gene therapy. My research on Alzheimer's was too broad."

"I see."

"Ms. Foreman, may I ask who your client is? And why you're interested in my early work?"

"I'm so sorry. I'm not at liberty to say."

"Hmm. You and the rest of the world."

"Excuse me?"

"You're not the first person to ask me about Alzheimer's recently."

"Really? Who else was interested?"

"I'm sorry. I'm not at liberty to say."

There was silence on the end of the phone. Then, Rachel said, "You have nothing to do with studying or working on the disease today, correct?"

"That's right."

"But you did, once upon a time."

"Correct."

A sigh. "I need to ask you to consider the rest of this conversation highly confidential, okay?"

"Well, it depends where it goes."

"I read your bio, and I know you do confidential work for the CDC, police departments all over the country, and even Homeland Security, so my request can't be a surprise."

He chuckled. "Like I said, you did your homework."

"My client has been working on a vaccine for Alzheimer's for years. Now it appears they are in danger of losing the formula to a third party. It would really help us if you could tell me who contacted you about Alzheimer's."

Hook drummed his fingers on his desk. Then he drummed them again. He'd enlisted in the Air Force, and seen action in Vietnam. Afterwards, there was Medical School and a PhD in human genetics. Research and teaching occupied most of his time, but he also consulted with governments, private industry, and other researchers. His loyalty was based on respect, and that included his government.

Then he thought about the coronavirus and how badly they had mismanaged it, bringing the country to a complete halt and prompting an ensuing economic depression. On top of that he was learning discovering that the people in charge of managing the virus were making money off the backs of sick Americans. Whether it was Senators racking in millions off insider trading or a President advocating an untested cure because he had a stake in the company that produced it, Hook was disgusted. Too many mornings, he woke up infuriated. This was not the country he knew and to which he'd given his loyalty. He was especially vexed by Homeland Security and the Justice Department who didn't lift a finger to stop the grifting and fraud.

Rachel asked, "Dr. Hookie, are you still there?"

"I am." He cleared his throat. "Now listen to me. I'm only going to say it once. I was called by an official from Homeland Security."

Rachel didn't answer right away. Then, she said, "Homeland Security?"

"I assumed the official was going to ask me something about the virus. But he asked me about Alzheimer's instead. He wanted to know if I knew about any ongoing secret clinical trials of a potential cure. I told him I didn't."

"What was his name?"

"His name was David Stearns."

Chapter 30

2:15 PM

David Stearns had been with Homeland Security for seven years, Rachel discovered online. Prior to that, he'd been a legislative aide to Congressman Hanover Newton, a Republican congressman from Kentucky, a physician turned politician. Stearns had grown up in Monsey, New York but moved when he was sixteen to attend American University in DC.

Rachel sucked in a breath. "Oh my god."

"What?" Zach asked.

"Monsey, New York has a huge population of ultra-Orthodox Jews. Hasidic. It's like West Rogers Park times twenty."

"Which means..."

"You know I'm Jewish, right?"

"I do. But I don't know anything about Hasidic Jews. Are they the ones who wear black wool suits even in summer, and those long sideburns?"

"Yup. They are very observant, very strict Jews. They came out of Eastern Europe in the 1800's. But they weren't like other Jews who came to America. They look different. They dress differently. They speak Yiddish. They brought their world with them, and refused to assimilate. We move forward in time. They move backwards."

"Sounds like a cult. Why so different?"

"Because they feel being different is the only way to be pious. Meanwhile, a lot of people think they're wildly hypocritical. The men study Torah all day while the women work. And cook. And take care of the kids. It's an inflexible, authoritarian, sexist world."

"Why?"

"Why what?"

"Why don't the men work?"

"Because their rebbes—they call them "rebbie" not rabbi— tell the men it's their holy duty to study Torah so they can grow closer to God. It's... well, don't get me started."

"You don't like them much, do you?"

"It's the women I don't understand. They get married at eighteen. They rarely go to college, although my grandfather says that's changing. And they're supposed to obey men who have no real world experience. They literally have no freedom. No wonder so many run away."

"Do they?"

"More and more. But if they're found, they can be forced to go back."

"You make it sound like prison."

"Well..."

"Is your grandfather one of them?"

"Not on your life. But he knows a few and respects their right to exist, I guess." Rachel bit her lip as though she wanted to say more but constrained herself.

"So, bottom line, what are you saying?"

"What I'm saying is that this Homeland Security guy, David Stearns, could have been raised Hasidic. But if you look at his LinkedIn photo, it's clear he isn't now."

"Hold on." Zach tapped some keys. "You're right. Brown hair, glasses, button down collar, jacket. He looks like an Ivy League prep."

"With a rep tie."

"You think he ran away?"

"I don't know, but we should find out. I'll call my grandfather. Maybe he can help. It could be important, you know?"

"Is it? Important?"

"The guy works for Homeland Security. He called Hookie, who hasn't studied Alzheimer's for thirty years, yet he asked if Hookie knew about any secret clinical trials of a cure."

Zach rubbed his chin. "Yeah. Maybe you should."

Rachel punched in a number on her phone. "Hi, Grampa."

"Hello, *Rah'chel*." Jake, Ellie's father, pronounced her name the Hebrew way with the 'ch' sound in the middle. "How's my favorite sweetheart?"

"I'm fine. I'm at work and I have a question."

"Shoot." Her grandfather was in his nineties, but he was still sharp. He lived in an assisted living home where he beat everyone at pinochle. And poker.

"Do you know anyone in Monsey, New York?"

"Oy. I used to. But I haven't talked to them in years. Decades. They're probably with Hashem now."

"I need a favor. Is there anyone up there you could call to get information about a boy—er, a man who grew up there?"

"Why?"

"I can't tell you, but Grampa, I really need your help."

He paused. Then, "Tell you what. I'll bet the rabbi at my shul knows someone up there. I'll ask him to call."

"It's got to be today. Right now, in fact."

"Well," Jake sniffed. "Good thing it's not Shabbos yet. I can try. What do you need to know?"

"Whether he grew up Hasidic and what happened to him."

Jake sighed. "Who and when?"

Rachel told him.

Jake called back in twenty minutes. "Well, well. This turned out to be an interesting story, *bubbala*."

"I'm listening."

"The thing is, like you, I'm not supposed to say anything about this young man either. Apparently, it was a real *shonda* for the community."

Rachel let out an impatient breath. Her grandfather liked to draw out conversations.

"David Stearns fled the community when he was sixteen. He claimed his father had been physically abusing him since he was eight. It was all supposed to be kept under wraps, but, of course, everyone knew in a New York minute." He chuckled at his own joke. "The family left Monsey, and the rebbe hasn't had any contact with them since. This happened a good twenty years ago, by the way."

"Did the son file a police report?"

"I'm sure he didn't. You know they rarely go outside the community."

"You are my hero, Grampa. Thank you! Please. Don't say anything about this, okay?"

"My lips are sealed."

Rachel disconnected and looked over at Zach who was tapping away on his computer. "You're not going to believe this, babe," he said.

"What?"

"While you were on the phone with your grandfather, I did a FRS on him."

"And?"

"Come here."

Zach had pulled up a news video from Charlottesville, Virginia, where in August 2017, violent clashes between neo-Nazi white nationalists and counter-protestors killed one woman and hospitalized six others in critical condition. The most iconic video was a nighttime march through the University of Virginia where the Neo-Nazis lit tiki-torches and chanted, "Jews will not replace us."

Zach had zoomed into a crowd of men, their faces lit by the torches. "Look at this guy."

Rachel squinted. The color drained from her face. "That's Stearns."

Chapter 31

"What do you want me to do with this?" LeJeune said.

"What do you mean?" Rachel replied.

"I mean, you don't have much. A guy works for Homeland. He's a Neo-Nazi. Frankly, he's not the only one over there. What does that have to do with Carefill's ransomware and the kidnapping?"

"He called one of his contacts, a man who used to work on Alzheimer's, and asked him directly if he'd heard anything about clinical trials of a cure."

"That's different. Why didn't you say so up front?"

"I did." *You weren't listening*, Rachel thought. "So this guy called a credible medical scientist with a question that indicates he knows something. We should take a closer look at him."

"I agree, *cher*. My mama always said I was *tête dur*. That means hard-headed."

Now he was apologizing and calling her "*cher*?"

Lejeune said, "We'll put eyes and ears on him, okay? That was fine work, Rachel. Hold on, your mother wants to talk to you."

"What's up, honey?" Ellie said.

Rachel explained and how Jake had called the *rebbe* in Monsey.

"Wow, you are one smart cookie. You're thinking he rebelled against his family so drastically that he became a Nazi?"

"As LeJeune says, he wouldn't be the first."

"Bobby Fischer," Ellie said.

"Huh?"

"The chess player. He hated Jews. Spewed constant venom about them until the day he died. The irony was that he was Jewish himself."

"Do you think it's possible," Rachel said, "that a group of anti-Semites are behind this?"

"That's a huge leap. Nick's right. Let's see what Stearns is up to."

"Mom, about Nick. I can't decide whether I like him or hate him."

"Sounds about right."

"What's your deal with him? And all those '*chers*'?"

"Not much. He helped me out during the Santoro case. Remember I had video outtakes of a guy asleep in the park at the same time he was supposedly murdering his girlfriend?"

"Not really. I was only thirteen."

"Right. Well, Nick thought we ought to hook up. I thought about it and declined the offer. He was and is a great FBI agent, but he isn't the most—dependable—man."

"That's all?"

"I was seeing David at the time."

"So you were fooling around?"

"No." Ellie said decisively. "Never."

"What about now?'

"Are you kidding? Luke is the only man in my life."

"Just checking."

"LeJeune is kind of full of himself. My take is he wants you to think he's a ladies man. You know the type."

"He isn't?"

"Who knows? More important, who cares? Like I said he's a great field agent. He and the agency helped us out when you were kidnapped, you know."

"No, I didn't."

"You had PTSD," her mother said gently. Then she changed the subject. "Hey, however this turns out, you and Zach are doing a great job. Stearns is a solid lead. I'll ask Pamela if she's heard of Dr. Hookie from Atlanta."

Chapter 32

3:00 PM

Pamela Cannon thought she was holding it together. She was grateful the FBI had stepped in, and she was pleased with the connections they were making. But the fact remained that her daughter had been kidnapped by whoever was attacking Carefill, and they were using her daughter's life as leverage. It was blackmail in its purest form, and her resolve to withstand the threat dwindled with each passing hour.

She'd been hard on herself for becoming a powerful business-woman. She'd stayed home with Laurie for two years after she was born. When she went back to work, she carved out time for soccer games and violin recitals, but she wasn't a PTA mother who spent her days playing tennis and fund-raising. On the affluent North Shore community in which they lived, that was tantamount to a sin worthy of excommunication.

The lingering doubt that she'd done the right thing with her daughter was always with her, and this morning it was growing expo-nentially. She'd pay whatever they asked for. The pain of never seeing her or hearing Laurie's voice on the phone again would sever her reason to live.

LeJeune counseled her to remain resolute. Under no circumstances should she release the formula for Alzheimer's. But he'd never had children. He didn't know the torment she was feeling.

Pamela stopped ruminating, roused herself, and went to the ladies room. After checking the stalls to be sure no one else was there, she faced herself in the mirror, taking in her bloodshot eyes, messy hair, and pale face. Her disheveled appearance was a sharp contrast to her normal buttoned-down precision. Fear and worry were evident even in her posture. For the first time, she had a vision of what she would look like as an old woman, bent over, only half-aware. She shuffled into a stall and broke down.

The door squeaked open. Someone else had come in.

The woman in the ladies room cleared her throat. "Pamela, it's Ellie."

Pamela's response was a strangled sob.

"There's no way you would know this, but about five years ago, Rachel was kidnapped. She was abducted by men impersonating the police. Right off the expressway."

Pamela was quiet for a moment. "I didn't know."

"It was—well, I can relate to what you're going through."

"How long was she a hostage?"

"Only two nights, but, of course, every minute felt like a month. I went crazy. I blamed myself."

"Like now."

Ellie nodded. "Somehow LeJeune and the FBI showed up. I don't remember how. I was in a fog. Anyway, he and the cops kept reminding me to have a stiff backbone. They didn't want me to yield, give them what they wanted. They kept saying as long as I didn't capitulate the other side wouldn't kill her. I didn't believe them. I wanted to give them what they wanted ASAP. Frankly, I don't know any mother who would think otherwise. We're wired that way. So I know what you're thinking. If it's a choice between Laurie or the formula, you're going to give them the formula, and fuck everything else."

"Are you saying that's the wrong thing to do?"

"How can I? I made the same decision."

Pamela came out of the stall, went to the sink, and washed her hands. The janitors had changed the soap to a floral-scented soap. She hated floral scents. "If it comes to that, will you help me?"

Ellie hesitated. She gazed at Pamela as if she understood the pain and anxiety digging deep lines on her face. "We still have eighteen hours to figure out who's behind this. And you have smart people working for you. Can you hold on until tomorrow morning?"

Pamela swallowed. "I don't know."

"If we don't crack this by then, we'll go to Plan B. Meanwhile, if you need to talk or cry or rant, I'm here."

Pamela leaned forward and squeezed Ellie's shoulder.

Chapter 33

4:00 PM

The heat and humidity felt like July, not May, as Rachel and Zach took a break to walk Joshua later that afternoon. A few minutes into the walk, sweat beaded the back of Rachel's neck. She was tired but still wired, which put her in a strange, jumpy but restless mood. She could tell Zach felt the same way. Even Joshua seemed to sense their stress and was subdued. They trudged around the tiny pond across from Zach's office trying to brainstorm their next steps.

LeJeune had called to tell them the Bureau got a warrant to tap Stearns' phone and track him by GPS. Apparently around three PM, he'd walked out of Homeland Security headquarters on Nebraska Avenue, stopped into a deli for take-out on Connecticut Avenue, and walked back down Nebraska to his office carrying a bag.

"Late lunch?" Zach asked on speakerphone.

"Don't know," LeJeune answered. "More important, we also found out he's been making calls to other Alzheimer's researchers and asking them about possible cures. And he's been to a couple of Alzheimer's conferences recently."

"That's pretty conclusive, isn't it?" Rachel said.

"Still circumstantial," LeJeune answered. "But it damn well warrants a closer look. Poke around, will you? See what else you can come up with. We will too."

"Of course," Rachel said.

"His title is Intelligence Analyst, but that can mean whatever they want it to."

Now, Rachel said, "What if I called Homeland? Pretended that I'm looking for a job? Asked what are the specific responsibilities of an Analyst?"

"It's already four. We don't have time," Zach slowed to let Joshua sniff the grass. "Plus it could be a made up title. You know, just for him. To cover his real work."

"Oh, you mean the way CIA agents are called diplomats in foreign countries?"

"Exactly. Your call might trip an alarm or something."

Rachel sighed. "Ok, your turn."

Zach pulled Joshua away from whatever he was scenting. "I'm thinking if he is part of a bigger plot, at some point he'll contact someone else who knows about it. Especially if they're responsible for the ransomware."

"You think he'll do it today?"

"The deadline is tomorrow morning."

"But this is most critical part of their plan. Wouldn't they be careful not to have any extraneous conversations? They've got to know we're trying to find them."

"Good point."

She was quiet for a moment. "So you're saying we have to wait for him to make a move. If he does."

"Anything else would probably be wasted energy."

"What about the Congressman he worked for? He was a doctor before he turned politician."

"The Bureau probably has a file on him, but we might be able to update it."

"Sounds like a plan," Rachel said.

They walked around the pond a second time with Rachel wilting from the heat. A roll of dirty gray clouds loomed in the western sky. "Looks like a storm's coming in."

Zach didn't answer. Rachel looked over. Zach was staring at the office building while Joshua did his business.

"What's wrong?"

"See that black SUV approaching the building?"

Rachel peered across the road and nodded.

The SUV coasted down the street. It slowed to a stop outside Zach's building. Two figures were in the front seat. Then it slowly rolled forward again.

"That's the third time that SUV has driven past." Zach looked at Rachel.

"Did you lock up before we left?" Rachel asked.

Zach nodded. "But we left the computers on."

"That's not good," she said. "Listen, I have an idea."

4:25 PM

A minute later they had the plate of the SUV, and a minute after that, they hurried into Rachel's Toyota. She drove east and then headed south on Sheridan Road toward Evanston. Zach called LeJeune with the plate number. He called back five minutes later. Zach put the call on speakerphone.

"It's a rental car. Hertz. I have someone checking their records. What are you doing?"

"We're stopping at my apartment for a minute," Rachel said.

"I have a feeling I know why, *cher*."

"You would be right, Nick."

"You be careful out there."

"I don't intend to use it."

"Hold on a minute." LeJeune said. Rachel listened to silence. LeJeune came back on. "Listen, Stearns just made a call to American University. Someone named Leonard Brandon. The call went to voicemail. Can you check him out?"

"Sure. Call you back."

When they arrived at Rachel's apartment, Zach hurried to Rachel's laptop lying on the kitchen counter and fired it up. Rachel went to her closet where she kept her Baby Glock. The Chicago Police Academy had required recruits get a Glock, and she'd chosen a sub-compact, nine millimeter, semi-automatic that held a ten-round magazine. She loved the pistol. It fit neatly in her hand, and the recoil wasn't bad. Plus it was small enough to easily conceal if needed. People said that Glocks didn't have safeties, but that wasn't entirely true. They didn't have a safety switch, but they did have a tab on the trigger that needed to be in a specific position or the gun wouldn't fire. That was good enough for Rachel.

She checked her gun to make sure it wasn't loaded, inhaling the weak but pleasant aroma—kind of like eggnog—of the G96 oil she used to clean and lubricate it. Then she took a loaded magazine out and slipped both into her bag. She walked back to Zach.

"Well?" she asked.

"This is weird," he said.

Rachel inclined her head.

"Professor Leonard Brandon is with the School of International Service, whatever that is. He teaches a course on America's relationship with far-right extremism and its movements, groups, and people."

"You're kidding."

Zach kept reading. "The course examines how 'nationalism' can be a cover for racist politics. Questions how successful right wing movements have been. Illustrates the patterns of right-wing extremist violence. And lays out how to confront the right wing nationalism on a federal level."

"That's crazy!" Rachel cried. "They actually have a course in how to become a right wing nut?"

"And what to expect from the Feds in response."

She crossed her arms. "Jesus. I know we have free speech, but this course takes it to a whole new level."

"Let's move on to Hanover what's-his-name. The Congressman. Stearns' former boss."

Zach opened Google and started scrolling. "Grew up in Louisville. Graduated from University of Kentucky. UT Southwestern Medical School in Dallas. Specialized in genetics. Practiced in—"

Rachel cut him off. "That was Hookie's specialty. You know, the Atlanta doctor. He went on to study Alzheimer's, too."

Zach looked up. "I would imagine lots of docs are interested in genetics. I mean, that's where all the action is now in terms of new drugs and things. Probably just a coincidence."

Rachel wasn't so sure. "Isn't he the guy who plays golf with the president all the time?" Zach tapped a few keys. "Sure is."

"Let's call in," she said.

Chapter 34

"So you're telling me this Professor teaches a class on white nationalism, how it started, what it does, how successful it is, and then teaches students how to rout it?"

"That's what it sounds like," Zach said to LeJeune, his cell on speakerphone.

"And David Stearns called him."

"Right."

"But the call went to Brandon's voicemail. Hold on..." LeJeune's voice grew muffled. He was talking to someone in the room. "No? Ok." His voice became crisp again. "Stearns didn't leave a message." He paused. "But he did call Hookie about a cure for Alzheimer's."

"Yup," Rachel answered this time. "And he went to all those Alzheimer's conferences."

"OK." LeJeune's voice was muffled again. "Boys and girls, we need another warrant. Professor Leonard Brandon. Let's get it ready." His voice cleared. "Good work, *cher*. Keep it up."

Zach cut in. "I love you too, Nick, but there's more. Stearns' former boss, Congressman Newman from Kentucky, is a doctor who once specialized in Alzheimer's. Turns out, he plays golf with the president."

"Is that so?" LeJeune said. "Looks like we might have the fixings for our own little Etouffee."

"Huh?" Zach said.

"Nothing. We'll start tracking their connections and communications. You guys can—"

"Did you find out who rented the SUV that was staking out my office?" Zach asked.

"John Smith. Fake address. Real credit card, though. We're still working on it."

"We're heading back that way, but if they're around, we'll have to make other arrangements." He glanced over at Rachel.

"Got it," LeJeune said.

Rachel glanced out her window. The storm had moved inland, bringing with it blinding rain, thunder, and lightning. "You drive."

They were quiet on the way back to Zach's office. Rachel broke the silence. "I don't get it. Why would right-wing anti-Semites and white nationalists, if they're the ones behind Laurie's kidnapping, want to steal an unproven cure for Alzheimer's? I can't make any sense of it."

"Because they can," Zach said. "They want to control the world from birth to death. What's that expression?"

"Cradle to grave," Rachel replied. "Maybe, maybe not. But they would want their leaders to be the only ones able to make critical decisions. And those leaders, naturally, would be old white men. I suppose if any of them were impaired—"

"That's it!" Zach said breathlessly. "You nailed it!"

"What?"

"One or more of those fuckers has Alzheimer's and they want the cure to bring whoever has it back to sanity."

Rachel was puzzled. "But—"

"But what?"

"Alzheimer's progresses slowly. Surely they would have time to train or promote someone new to take his place."

"Yeah, but what if that person was so important to their cause they'd go to any length to cure him?"

"Zach, that's crazy. That's like saying they'd do anything to cure Hitler." Rachel paused for a moment. Then she clapped her hand over her mouth. "Oh my god."

Zach was on a roll. "You know how Alzheimer's patients have moments of mental clarity?"

Rachel nodded.

"So what if, during one of those moments, he or she ordered them to find a cure for himself? How could they refuse?"

"But it's insane! And unbelievably risky. What if they were caught? Arrested. Convicted of blackmail, theft, and kidnapping/ Not to mention treason and sedition. Their entire movement would be destroyed."

Zach didn't answer for a moment. Then, "Tell me something. When has that stopped a president who thinks he's got 'total authority'?"

Chapter 35

5:55 PM

The pounding rain sounded like machine gun fire as they parked Rachel's car in front of Zach's office building. The streetlights, dim and useless in the fog of the storm, had come on, but they didn't reveal any strange SUVs. Rachel and Zach sprinted to the door of the building, Joshua in tow, but were soaked by the time they hurried down the hall to Zach's office.

The sight that greeted them could have been something out of a Bruce Willis movie. Zach's office door was thrown open. Nothing happened when Zach flicked the overhead light switch, but light from the hall and windows spilled in enough for them to see that everything was obliterated. His four computers smashed, their parts hurled across the floor. Circuit boards torn apart. Jagged shards of glass from his monitors lay like a glittering dangerous carpet. Chairs upside down. His conference table chopped into pieces. A slight burnt rubber smell drifted through the air.

Terror crackled up Rachel's back, and she pulled out her Glock. Zach was frozen, and it wasn't until Joshua whined that he bent down to pet the dog.

"Wait!" Rachel whispered. "They may be in the other room." She didn't wait for Zach's reply but hurried to the door to the back room, took a breath, and centered herself. As she threw open the door, she crouched and assumed a shooting position.

No one was there. "We're safe."

Slowly, she stood, holstered her gun, and walked back over to Zach. He grabbed a flashlight from a drawer to survey the damage. The beam illuminated one pile of detritus after another.

"Oh god! I'm so sorry, Zach." She slipped her arms around him and rested her head on his shoulder.

"Hey, sweetie, don't worry. We're okay, and some of my data might be in the cloud, so I can get it back. Best of all, the machines are insured." Then he made a sound that was A half cry, half laugh. "You think they were sending us a message?"

6:30 PM

With no computers or electricity in the office, they fed Joshua, put him in the back seat, and picked up Wendy's for dinner. Rain lashed the car windows, and lightning and thunder still rumbled, but lunchtime seemed a long time ago, and Rachel was famished. Wolfing down hamburgers and fries in the car, Zach said, "I need to be hands-on if we're going to do anything more."

"What about my laptop?"

"It doesn't have the apps I need."

"You think we could 'borrow' one of the Cyber Division's computers? It probably has more bells and whistles than yours."

"Maybe, but that would be my last resort. The Bureau might force me to get approvals from the higher-ups for things I'd rather do on my own. You know what I mean?"

Rachel nodded and stuffed a bunch of fries into her mouth. After she swallowed them she said, "Hey, didn't you do a big project for Georgia Davis last year? Something about going through a Facebook group to get identities?"

"How did you know about that?"

"Word gets around." Rachel grinned. "But the point is that you've got a lot of pals who are white hat hackers."

"Red ones, too."

"Even better. Why can't we go to one of them and use their gear?"

Zach considered it. "I suppose that would be okay, considering the circumstances."

"What are friends for anyway?" A crash of thunder punctuated her comment. "See? Even the guy upstairs agrees with me."

Zach smiled for the first time that night.

Chapter 36

Ten minutes later they drove down to Skokie and parked in front of a small apartment building on Greenleaf Street. Rachel called LeJeune to tell him what happened at Zach's office and where they were. He sounded actually cheerful.

"Sorry to hear that. I'm sure Carefill will help replace your equipment."

"He says it's insured. But tell me why you sound so jolly."

"We think we've identified two more people associated with what we're calling the cabal."

"Oh?"

"Not sure I want to be too specific on my cell."

"Oh. What do you need from us?"

"Help us find the hacker for the group."

"On it," Rachel said.

"Rachel, your momma sends love and says she hopes you're being careful."

Rachel smiled. "Tell her I am. I hope she is, too."

~

They climbed out of the car, walked Joshua, and arrived at Zach's friend soaking wet. After Zach rang the bell, a nasal voice came through the intercom.

"Hey, Wookie. It's Zach, Rachel, and Joshua."

Rachel arched her eyebrows and mouthed "Wookie?"

"You brought the party!"

"Always. Do you have a couple of towels?"

"Towels? Is this a new party game? Or are you just wet?"

"Come on, man, let us up."

The door buzzed and they walked up to the third floor. Wookie met them with three dishtowels. Like the Star Wars character, he was tall and had bristly eyebrows, but his shoulder length brown hair was thicker, shaggier, and more tousled than Chewbacca's.

"Rachel, Wookie," Zach introduced them.

"Hi, Wookie."

He nodded and looked her over. "I approve."

"You already know Joshua," Zach said.

Wookie bent down to pet the dog. "We're two of a kind, aren't we, Joshie?"

"So pal, you've got Recorded Future and Kali Linux, right?"

Wookie straightened up. "I do."

"What's Recorded Future?" Rachel asked.

Wookie glanced at Zach, who gave him a brief nod. "It's a threat intelligence program. It can discover, screen, and analyze threats in real time with the power of hundreds of humans."

"AI," Zach added.

"This I want to see," Rachel said.

"Follow me and we will time warp to another galaxy," Wookie said.

Wookie led them into a room that looked like a smaller version of Zach's office. There were two desktops and a laptop, three large monitors, and the same jumble of cables, wires, and smaller boxes Rachel was just learning about. Zach sat down in front of one computer.

Rachel was about to pull up a chair from the other machine when a sudden crack of thunder startled her. She whipped her head toward the window.

"Some storm, huh?" Wookie said. Rachel nodded. "Well, I'll let you two do your thing. If you need me I'll be in the other room watching Netflix."

"Thanks, man," Zach said. "I really appreciate it."

Wookie smiled, then closed the door, leaving them alone.

Rachel turned to Zach. "Actually, there's something I've been wondering about."

"What's that, babe?"

"The problems for Cannon started with Morgan and Warner. Fields met them on the dark web after Cannon fired him for embezzling money."

"Right."

"But this second group, who seem to be way more sophisticated and dangerous than Morgan, penetrated Carefill's system by sending Fields that threatening email."

"Yeah?"

"So, how did they know Fields was embezzling money in the first place? They obviously knew *before* he was fired."

"Good question. I suppose they ran across some emails or texts between Cannon and her executive team discussing what Fields was doing."

"Yeah, but how did the hacker get in? You said it took months to take control of a system."

"Email is different," Zach said. "Remember I've got a password cracker in Kali Linux. I would assume the hacker for this group has it, too. He probably got into their personal computers—you know, Pamela's and the other two guys. When he figured out Fields was vulnerable, he sent Fields that phishing email and was able to penetrate Carefill's system."

"Talk about a stroke of luck," Rachel said.

"You can say that again." Zach rubbed his chin. "After that, he probably tracked every move Fields made. Followed him to the dark web, watched him hook up with Morgan. Probably tracked Morgan and the woman, too."

"So the cabal could kill them after *they* killed Fields."

"Big fish swallows little fish," Zach shrugged. "And now we're doing some fishing of our own." He sighed. "Except I've got no idea where to drop our line."

Rachel pulled up a chair and sat. "Then it's a good thing I do."

7:43 PM

"You know how illegal drug dealers get fentanyl and the ingredients for meth on the dark web?" Rachel said.

"Yeah?" Zach left the word hanging.

"Well, earlier today I learned that pharmaceutical drugs have to be manufactured in a certain order to ensure the formula works. There are precise steps that have to be followed. For example, some ingredients are heat sensitive. Others aren't. You have to use the precise concentration of a substance. And if you have the wrong binder, or other ingredient, it will work against the formula."

Zach rubbed the back of his neck. "You're talking Greek. So?"

"So, the cabal would need to do some testing before they actually gave it to the person or people for whom it was designed. Not a lot. Just enough to make sure they were making it properly."

"You're saying that even if they had the formula, they can't just whip up a batch and use it right away."

Rachel nodded. "It's not like a recipe where you mix everything together and throw it into the oven. They'd have to know how to follow the steps in order."

"What kind of tests are you talking about?"

"I'm thinking they'd need at least a few Alzheimer's patients to volunteer to take the new medication."

"All this to save a few power-hungry Nazis who want to rule the world? But you're right. It makes sense. Who would turn down the opportunity to see their loved ones recover?"

"Exactly. Maybe the group already knows a few of the ingredients they're going to need. Common things, like capsules or fillers. Or maybe they know one or two of the actual ingredients that are apt to be part of the cure. Is there a way you can see if anyone has been shopping for those ingredients?"

"That's a brilliant idea. But what ingredients am I looking for?"

Rachel raised her index finger, pulled out her cell, and called her mother.

Chapter 37

E llie went into Pamela Cannon's office and closed the door.
"What's going on?" Pamela looked haggard and miserable.
Ellie wasn't sure how much longer she would last. The anxiety of
knowing her daughter's life was on the line because of her career had
to be unbearable. She knew all too well.

"I need you to tell me a couple of the most common ingredients
in the Alzheimer's formula."

Pamela jerked her head up, suspicion clouding her eyes. "What?
Why?"

Ellie explained Rachel's theory. "Whoever this group is, this
"cabal," they might be looking for some of the more common ingredients on the dark web. So that they're ready to test it once you give
them the formula. You don't have to reveal anything that's part of the
'secret sauce.' Just some of the more common components."

That got a raised eyebrow from Pamela.

"Rachel was thinking capsules or fillers. If we can find someone is
stocking up on certain items, it could help narrow down who's
behind this."

"You can track supplies like that?" Pamela seemed doubtful.

"They're going to try."

Pamela shook her head. "Why can't the FBI pick up the two or three people they already suspect? Pressure them to confess." For the first time, Ellie thought, Cannon sounded like a CEO. Arrogant and determined to get her own way.

Ellie paused. "You know the answer to that, Pamela. Your daughter's life would be in more jeopardy than it is now."

Pamela stared at Ellie for what seemed like a full minute. Her composure returned, and she reluctantly said, "Please ask Devin and Stan to come in, will you?"

8:15 PM

Zach went to work on Wookie's computer, tapping keys, looking at his monitor, and making notes on paper. Rachel's mother had given them a list of five ingredients:

Cholinesterase inhibitors: Current medications like Donepezil, Galantamine, Rivastigmine, and Memantine, used with Alzheimer's patients to prevent the breakdown of acetycholine in the brain, which promotes memory, alertness, thought, and judgment.

ODTs: orally disintegrating tablets that dissolve quickly in the mouth and are used in the above medications

Gelatin Empty Capsules

Bulking agents (fillers or diluents): substances formulated alongside the active ingredient of a medication, included for long-term stabilization, bulking up active ingredients in small amounts

VX-765, a particular Caspase-1 inhibitor that some researchers say has an unprecedented beneficial effect in Alzheimer mice. The drug rapidly reverses memory loss, eliminates inflammation, and stops

Alzheimer's prototypical amyloid peptide accumulation in the mice brains.

The first thing Zach did was a search of the ingredients for sale on the dark web. He found over a dozen sources selling one or more of the substances.

When he told Rachel, she stood and started to pace. "So many? I guess I shouldn't be surprised."

Slowly he picked out would-be customers by their usernames. Then he tried to identify them by using a combination of applications, mostly Recorded Future and Google Analytics. To be honest, Rachel wasn't sure what he was doing.

"Are you ranking them?" she asked. "And if so, how?"

"Partly by their usernames. Partly by their location. Partly by hunch."

"Hunch?"

"Hunch backed up by AI. It's complicated. Google can tell me that the same machine logged into Location A and then into location B. Recorded Future can give me indications of where they are and what Internet provider they're using. Between them both, I'll eventually get an IP address. Provided it's not spoofed and we're lucky, we'll be able to tell the FBI 'we think it came from this IP address, using this Internet provider, logging into sites in Philadelphia, DC, and Santa Clara,' for example. They'll take it from there." He let out a breath. "But it's going to take time. It's a process of elimination. I have over a hundred usernames to check out."

"We've got all night," Rachel said hopefully. She gazed out Wookie's window. At least the storm had moved out. A steady rain persisted, but it wasn't intense.

"Let's hope that's enough time." Zach's voice was grim.

10:30 PM

Two hours later, another storm front moved in. Rain fell sideways in sheets, and the wind kicked up, dropping tree branches, shrieking at windows, and blowing everything that wasn't tied down.

Zach had made some progress, but not enough. He'd eliminated seven potential buyers who'd contacted the websites. "Only ninety-three left."

Rachel stood up to massage his neck.

He looped his arms backwards around her waist.

"I wish I could do something to help," she said.

"You're here. That's enough."

Suddenly a fork of lightning split the sky. It was followed by a crack like a gunshot. Then everything went dark.

Chapter 38

10:35 PM

Rachel jumped at the sound. "Jesus! What was that?"

"The transformer blew."

"Are you sure?"

Wookie opened the door. "You guys okay? Check your cells." He held his up. "Mine's working." He came in, followed by Joshua, who padded up to Zach and nuzzled his head on Zach's lap. Wookie clicked on his cell's flashlight and beamed the light from Zach to Rachel. "Sorry. This is one hell of a storm."

Rachel took a deep breath to calm down. "We're screwed, aren't we?"

Zach pulled out his cell and a business card. Using his flashlight to read, he punched in a phone number. "There's always Plan B."

10:45 PM

Ten minutes later, they were back in Rachel's car. The storm was already moving out, as if it had finally spent itself and was exhausted. They dropped Joshua at Rachel's place, then headed for

Lake Shore Drive and downtown Chicago. Light traffic on the Drive helped them get to FBI headquarters on Roosevelt Road in half an hour.

"You sure this is what you want to do?" Rachel asked as they parked and climbed out of the car. She breathed in the sweet musty scent of rained-on concrete as they headed down the sidewalk.

"We're out of options, and he said he could help."

"Forrester?"

Zach nodded.

"I didn't know you and he were buddies."

"We're not. But we did talk at Carefill this morning."

"Seems like weeks ago."

"Tell me about it. Anyway, on the phone just now, he said he has Recorded Future and a program that's even more powerful. That's gonna be awesome." Zach's expression was eager and excited, like a kid anticipating his Christmas present.

Rachel flashed him a smile. She hoped the present lived up to his expectations.

11:25 PM

The security approval process at FBI headquarters was surprisingly relaxed, Rachel noted. Picture IDs, fingerprints, but nothing else. Carl Forrester met them in the lobby, talked to security, then motioned to a bank of elevators. They ascended to an upper floor.

The Cyber Division occupied the entire floor, but it looked anachronistic, as if the space had been the Bureau's IT Department fifteen years earlier, which Forrester admitted it was. One room contained the tall metal stacks and shelves of a mainframe system and servers. The rest of the floor was occupied by standard office cubicles. Although it was almost midnight, most of the cubicles were filled with FBI nerds who probably were spying on everyone in the universe.

Forrester set Zach up in an empty cubicle. Rachel assumed she would sit with him, but when Forrester saw her pull up a chair, he shook his head. "LeJeune wants you back at Carefill's headquarters," he said.

"Why?"

"I don't know, but a car's waiting downstairs."

Rachel hugged Zach and whispered. "Good luck. Keep me updated. See you soon."

Zach nodded and sat at the desk. He looked like he'd just opened his present and couldn't wait to play.

Midnight

When Rachel arrived back at Carefill, she was relieved to see her mother still there. She hurried over and gave her a hug.

"What's that for?" Ellie asked with a smile.

Rachel was just realizing the pressure she was under: pressure to solve problems, make decisions, and make sure they were followed up. That wasn't inherently a bad thing; in fact, it was what Rachel had always hoped for in a job. LeJeune, Zach, even Pamela Cannon seemed to respect her input. But seeing her mother felt like a temporary reprieve from all the stress. She could bounce things off her mom and listen to her mother's advice. She recalled the old story about the college graduate who was amazed how much his parents had learned in four years.

"I'm just glad to see you," Rachel said. "So what are you doing?"

"Mostly waiting." Ellie paused. "You?"

Rachel filled her in.

"You've been all over the place."

"Seems like it."

"Well, take a load off. Maybe even catch a nap."

"Are you kidding? No way."

"Then grab some coffee. I just made a pot." Ellie motioned to a coffee machine in the back of the conference room.

Rachel was pouring coffee when LeJeune came in. "Good, you're back."

She turned around. "Why am I here instead of FBI headquarters? I wanted to stay with Zach."

"Honestly? I need Zach to concentrate one hundred and fifty percent."

Rachel bristled. "You're assuming I'm a distraction?"

LeJeune stopped, as if he knew he'd said the wrong thing. "Not at all, Rachel. But Carl assigned two men to work with him. It's better that you're here."

"And not in their way."

Her mother spoke up. "Rachel, not now, okay? We're all on edge."

Rachel turned back to LeJeune. "Sorry. It's been a long day."

"It's gonna be an even longer night, *cher*."

Chapter 39

A t LeJeune's request, Rachel called Zach to see how they were proceeding. The deadline to turn over the formula was seven hours away.

"How's it going?" she asked.

He cleared his throat. "We've removed about two dozen usernames. Either their location or their IP addresses, after we identify them, tell us they aren't the ones. We have a couple of possibilities, but we still have over sixty or seventy to go."

"You've got two guys helping you, right?"

"Yup. But this just isn't a quick process, babe."

"I understand. Do you have any kind of time estimate?"

"I know when the deadline is. But honestly, I don't know when we'll finish."

Rachel told LeJeune what Zach said. LeJeune called Forrester and asked him to add more cyber security experts to Zach's team. Forrester replied there weren't any others at the moment who were proficient enough with the apps they were using.

LeJeune barked into the phone. "Find some."

Both Ellie and Rachel whipped around. Ordinarily LeJeune was mild-mannered and affable, the epitome of the laid-back FBI agent.

Not tonight.

4:46 AM

When Rachel checked in again, Zach said they were about halfway through. Forrester was now working with him, and somehow he'd found another agent who knew enough to be useful.

"You sound more optimistic."

"There's always hope," he said.

"You're a trooper."

After the call, Rachel yawned and lay down on the couch in the conference room and closed her eyes.

6:32 AM

When she opened them again, she was alone. Her mother was gone. So was LeJeune. Rachel got up, stretched, and went to the ladies room to wash her face and brush her hair. On her return she heard voices coming from Pamela's office. The door was closed. She sat at Kelly's desk. Pamela's assistant must be in her boss's office. Maybe LeJeune too—she thought she heard his voice—and her mother.

Five minutes later the door opened and LeJeune, Kelly, and her mother filed out. LeJeune was on his phone. When her mother saw Rachel, she gestured for Rachel to follow her. They went back into the conference room.

"It's not looking good."

Rachel stiffened. "What's going on?"

"They still have about thirty usernames to research."

Rachel checked the time on her cell. With only two and a half hours remaining, the deadline was looming. "What are you going to do?"

Ellie shrugged. "It's not clear yet."

LeJeune slipped his cell back in his pocket and walked over.

"Pamela's calling Devin and Stan. They're the ones who know where the formula is."

Rachel frowned. "Isn't it locked in a safe someplace that only a few people know about?"

LeJeune shook his head. "That's not the way it works anymore. They divided the formula into several pieces, then took each piece and electronically sent it to a different server. Any server. That way, no one can break into headquarters and physically or electronically steal the whole thing."

Rachel rubbed her arm with her other hand. "But wouldn't the cabal—if that's what we're dealing with—have found it once they took control of Carefill's network?"

"No. They don't know which servers the pieces are on. Could be Google, could be Amazon, could be a private server in—in Norway," LeJeune said. "If we don't find their chief hacker by nine, that's what Pamela has to tell them. Where the formula is on all the servers." He rubbed his eyes. "I've got agents standing by all over the country, and Interpol's waiting in Europe, but I'm not sanguine about our prospects, *mes chers.*"

Chapter 40

K elly came into the conference room. "Ellie, Pamela wants to see you in her office."

Ellie rose, threw Rachel a puzzled look, and followed Kelly.

Rachel called Zach. "Where are you?"

"Five more to go. Three potential buyers. But we also have to face the possibility that we're totally off base, and they didn't go to the dark web to buy supplies. This may have been a complete waste of time."

"No. No it isn't. We had no choice."

Zach sighed. "Well, I'm sure that'll be open to discussion after the fact. I wish you were here, babe."

"I wish I was too."

8:33 AM

Ellie went into Pamela's office. Devin and Stan were with her, but Pamela shooed them out. "I need a few minutes alone with Ellie."

Ellie sat in the chair Devin had just vacated. The seat was warm.

Pamela, drawn and pale, was a mess. Her hair needed brushing, her clothes were wrinkled, and fine lines around her mouth had appeared. But it was her morose expression that alarmed Ellie.

"I've written a letter of resignation," Pamela said. "I'll deliver it to the Board of Directors after the phone call."

"You can't," Ellie said. "This is not over."

Pamela pointed to a clock on the wall. "Ellie, look at the time. It's not going to happen. My daughter is everything to me. I can't—I won't risk her life."

Ellie sucked in a breath. "In the ladies room a few hours ago, you said you might need my help."

Pamela shook her head. "There's nothing you can do. I realize that now."

"You're right, there's nothing I can do. But you can."

Pamela inclined her head. "What are you talking about?"

"Do you know who Charlotte Hollander is?"

Pamela frowned, revealing deep lines across her forehead. "The name is familiar."

"She was VP and Chief of Engineering at Delcroft Airlines."

"Yes." Pamela's forehead smoothed out. "I know her. I've seen her at a couple of PAC meetings."

"I watched her do exactly what I'm going to suggest to you. It worked."

Chapter 41

P amela's phone rang promptly at nine. Seven people had congregated in the CEO's office: the two Carefill executives, LeJeune, Rachel, Ellie, and Kelly. The same robotic voice as the first time said, "Good morning, Pamela. Have you decided?"

Rachel looked at the clock. If Zach called within the next ten seconds, they could still save the formula. She checked her cell. No call.

Despite a sleepless night, Pamela's voice was firm. "I have. I am prepared to turn over the formula after I see proof that my daughter is alive and healthy."

"A wise decision, Pamela," the voice said. "One moment."

Static came over the line. Then silence followed by a click, as if the connection had been transferred. A feminine voice came on. "Mom?"

"Laurie, are you all right? Are you being treated well?"

"I can't talk right now. I want to see you. Maybe we could meet in Frankfurt after this is—"

Laurie's voice was cut off by a male voice crying "*Scheisse!*", followed by a loud swish on her end, as if the phone was being passed from one person to another.

"She's in Frankfurt!" LeJeune said. "I'll be back." He hurried out of the room.

At the same time, Rachel's cell trilled. She checked her phone. Zach! "What's happening?" she asked breathlessly.

"We got him."

"Who and where?"

"His user name is *Dark Knight*. And he's in Kentucky. Louisville."

"He's in the US?"

"Tell LeJeune. Have his agents go to..." He reeled off a street address in Louisville.

"But LeJeune thinks they're in Frankfurt, Germany."

"It doesn't matter. What's going on with the call?"

"It's happening now."

"Oh no. Crap."

"Hold on." Rachel left the room. LeJeune was on his cell, talking and waving his other hand in the air. She raised up her phone and mouthed, "Zach!"

LeJeune snatched her phone. "What did you find?" He listened. "Maryland Avenue? That's the Highlands. Affluent neighborhood." Silence. "OK." He disconnected and gave her back her cell. "You go back into the office. I've only got a few minutes." He lifted his cell to his ear and resumed his conversation.

Rachel slipped back into Pamela's office. Pamela was talking into the speakerphone. "As you likely know, the formula was dispersed to several different servers. We have retrieved all the pieces. They're all on a piece of paper I'm holding in my hand. But before I hand it over, I have questions. How will I know my daughter has been released? When will our network be unlocked? And how will we know you are no longer in our system?"

"Your daughter will be dropped off at the Kempinski Hotel in Frankfurt within the hour. But tell the FBI it will be a waste of Interpol's time to look for us. We are not there. Your system will be restored by noon your time. As for your third question, there is no guarantee. But once we have the formula, our interest in your business will cease."

And Carefill will have much more powerful firewalls, Rachel thought.

"How would you like to receive the formula?" Pamela asked

The voice told her to hold the paper up to the camera on her computer. She did. The camera at the top of her monitor flashed green, stayed on for about thirty seconds, then flashed off.

"I need to talk to my daughter again. Just to make sure she's okay."

But the voice was gone.

Chapter 42

An hour later, as promised, Interpol reported the arrival of Laurie Cannon at the Kempinski in Frankfurt. The FBI had arranged for a suite, and a physician was waiting to examine her. A female agent would protect her until she was on her way to the States.

Pamela's anxiety, however, didn't ebb until she was able to talk to Laurie. Her captors, two men who wore masks, had treated her well. The only exception was the abduction itself, when they forced her into an unmarked van near the World Bank as she returned from lunch. Inside the van they blindfolded her and tied her down on the middle seats.

Interpol and the FBI interviewed Laurie to see if she could tell them where she'd been held. She told them they'd left Brussels and had been in the van all afternoon; she could tell it was dusk by the time they arrived at their destination. She was led into some kind of warehouse. When they took off her blindfold, she saw it had been equipped with a sofa bed, a lamp, and a chair. A tiny bathroom that reeked of stale urine and feces occupied a corner. The room had windows that were covered by shades and some kind of black protective wire on the outside, but at one point she spotted the truck of a beer distributor with an address ending in "Frankfurt, Germany" through a crack in a shade. Frankfurt was a four-hour drive from Brussels.

9:53 AM

A SWAT team from the FBI's Louisville Field Office raided a stately red brick home with white columns in the Bonnycastle neighborhood. Sweeping aside a frightened African-American housekeeper, they searched the house and found a young man in a small gun room in the basement. He was attempting to disable an impressive array of electronic equipment that included several computers, monitors, as well as a built-in camera, printer, scanner, and other gear that they later discovered was part of a cyber security system.

The young man was Bruce Newton, son of Congressman Hanover Newton from Kentucky. Newton's wife and son had remained in Kentucky after the Congressman was elected ten years earlier so that his son could finish college. Instead Bruce, a ne'er do well now well into his thirties, discovered a lucrative career as a hacker.

The Washington Field Office rounded up the Congressman, who promptly hired an attorney and offered to roll over and tell the FBI everything in return for a non-prosecution agreement for himself and his son.

LeJeune flew to D.C. where Newton made his proffer.

"I've become close to the President over the past few years," he said to several FBI officers and attorneys seated around a conference table. "We have a lot in common. Ideologically and personally."

"Do you know David Stearns?" LeJeune asked.

"Stearns is a friend of my son, Bruce," the Congressman replied in a bland tone.

"How did they meet?"

"In Charlottesville."

LeJeune arched a brow. "What about Professor Leonard Barton??"

"Stearns knew him. Leonard found the German scientist, an Alzheimer's specialist who we worked with."

"Worked with? How exactly?"

Newton cleared his throat. "The President was diagnosed almost a year ago. Everyone knew it was coming. It was the worst kept secret in D.C. During his lucid moments, he demanded that doctors and scientists find a cure for him." He glanced at everyone in the room. "He tasked me with handling the 'project.'"

LeJeune wasn't sure if Newton was proud or ashamed.

"And you did this out of the goodness of your heart? Because you're so fond of the President?"

Newton went on. "Hell no. He promised there would be a lot of new campaign donations rolling in. I said to fuck the donations. We wanted a percentage of the profits." Newton paused. "He agreed."

"How did you hear about Carefill's involvement?"

"The Alzheimer's community isn't that large. Erich, over in Frankfurt, heard some rumors and did some digging. Turned out the rumors were true. We knew the company would never test it on the President of the United States, so we came up with another approach."

"To steal it."

Newton shrugged.

"And you headed up the operation?"

Newton shook his head. "Only nominally. Everyone had an equal role. It took almost a year to put the plan in motion." He paused. "You know the rest."

"Who spoke on the phone to Ms. Cannon?"

"It was Bruce." Newton looked proud.

"Who prepped him?"

"We all did. True, it was an audacious plan. Bold. Risky. But if we succeeded, we would all be rich beyond measure, including the President. The market for an Alzheimer's cure is nearly fifty billion dollars."

"Except you weren't going to distribute it to everyone."

Newton shifted. "What are you talking about?"

"You were going to restrict its availability to right-wing racists. No people of color. No immigrants. Just old shitheads like yourselves."

"That's not true. One member of our team is a Jew."

"We have video of 'this Jew' at Charlottesville. He's carrying a Nazi sign."

Newton straightened. "Then you know his history. It was a bad business between him and his father. We took him in."

"Why?"

"Why what?"

"Why perpetrate an assault on human decency by restricting one of the most miraculous drugs mankind has ever designed?"

"Some miracle." Newton scoffed. "The elderly live too long. Whether they have Alzheimer's or some other health malady. And they *all* have health maladies. They drain the healthcare system. Medicare's on life support, and the country can't afford it."

"But you were going to produce it anyway. For a select market and screw the rest. And make yourselves wildly rich in the process." LeJeune said coldly. "Tell me, how was that *your* decision to make?"

"It wasn't." For the first time Newton looked uncomfortable.

"Whose was it?"

"Who do you think?"

Chapter 43

A week later, Pamela Cannon hosted a private dinner at the Peninsula Hotel downtown. Just Cannon, her daughter Laurie, LeJeune, Zach, Rachel and Ellie. Cannon ordered a bottle of champagne. When it arrived and everyone's glasses were full, Cannon made a toast.

"To the 25th Amendment of the Constitution."

"Hear, hear," Ellie replied. "Let's hope the Vice-President can unify the country."

"Or at least keep the corruption at bay," Laurie said. "Who knows? If he succeeds, I might have to move back to the States."

Pamela beamed. "That would be wonderful."

Rachel thought Laurie looked like a younger version of her mother: blond, fit, and intelligent. "How long will you be staying?"

Laurie smiled. "Until Mom and I are sick of each other."

Cannon looked at her watch. That got a laugh. Then she said, "Seriously, none of this would have been possible without all of your help. I am, and will be, forever in your debt."

Ellie spoke up. "You have every reason to count yourself among us, you know."

If it were possible for the CEO of a Fortune 500 company to

blush, Rachel was sure Pamela was doing just that. "What do you mean, Mom?"

Ellie said, "To use a metaphor Zach and Nick will appreciate, it was Pamela who pushed us over the five yard line."

Pamela demurred. "Now, Ellie, I thought—"

Her mother cut in. "This is a woman with guts." She looked around. "What I'm going to tell you is strictly confidential." She grinned. "Nick."

LeJeune raised his hands in a surrender gesture. "You've got it."

"As you know, a formula is like a recipe. It lists the elements—the ingredients—but if you don't know how and when to combine them, it won't work." She glanced at Pamela. "And if you happen to forget one, well, you have... nothing but a mess on your hands."

"Is that what you did, Pamela?" Rachel asked.

"Your mother suggested it."

Rachel looked at her mother with newfound respect. "That was pretty risky."

"No riskier than giving a flash drive to a bad guy to get my daughter back."

"There was nothing on the drive?" Zach asked.

"There was plenty on it," Ellie said and smiled at Rachel. "But that's another story. Bottom line, whatever Carefill surrendered to the group of white men was useless. It won't work."

The waiter took their appetizer orders and disappeared.

"You know, I might be off base here," Rachel said, "But I was thinking about David Stearns and the Hasidic community. And how closed off they are from the rest of the world."

"What about it?"

"Wasn't he just as closed off from the world when he became a neo-Nazi?"

"It's not the same thing," Ellie said. "One group worships God in a benign way; the other is nothing more than a greedy collection of right-wing crazies."

"But they're both cults, aren't they?" Rachel persisted.

"It may look that way," Ellie went on. "But, in my opinion, there's a difference. The tragedy is that David Stearns was a victim who ended up on the wrong side."

No one said anything. Rachel wasn't convinced Stearns was a victim, but she'd take that issue up with her mother and grandfather another time.

Zach broke the silence. "What's going to happen to the rest of the 'cabal'?"

"After we finish investigating, you can bet there will be a slew of charges," LeJeune said. "Extortion, kidnapping, blackmail, not to mention corporate theft. Oh, and, I hear D.C. rejected Newton's proffer. He'll be charged along with his son."

"It's too bad about Bruce Newton," Zach said. "He could just as easily have been a good guy. You know, a white hat. He was central command of an op that spanned Germany, Louisville, DC, and Chicago. A lot of careful planning went into it."

Everyone groaned.

"Bad joke, Zach," LeJeune laughed.

"I'm serious."

"I know," LeJeune said. "I am too. I want you to know you have a job at the Bureau whenever you want. I can send you both to Quantico tomorrow."

Rachel and Zach looked at each other. She remembered Zach saying how much he prized his independence. After working this case, she too could see the benefits of remaining on the outside. But she didn't want to offend anyone.

"Can we let you know?" she asked. "We'll give it careful consideration."

ACKNOWLEDGMENTS

I owe a debt of thanks to Uvi Ponansky for inviting me to contribute to the High-Tech Crime Solvers linked series of novels. I've never done that before, and it's been fun, especially incorporating a character from another author's series, in this case Barbara Ebel's, whose "Hookie" ended up becoming the driving force in my story.

Also many thanks to Fred Bedrich, a Canadian cyber security expert who patiently explained in layman's terms some of the software and apps described in this novel. Any mistakes or misinterpretations are due to my own ignorance in this arena as well as my medical knowledge, or lack thereof.

To those who read it and contributed suggestions, thank you. That would include Tim Chapman, Eric Arnall, Cara Black, Kent Krueger, Judy Bobalik, Steve Finkelmeyer, and Pam Elliot. I am grateful for your time and your friendship. And, thanks to Sue Trowbridge, who can make anything look professional and attractive.

I hope you enjoyed the read.

They say word-of-mouth is the best sales tool in the world. If you enjoyed *Virtually Undetectable,* I would love it if you let your friends know. "They," whoever they are, also say reviews are the lifeblood for authors (forgive the pun). I'd be grateful if you left a review on the site where you bought the book, Goodreads, or another platform.